LIGHTS IN THE SKY

WINSTON GAMBRO

ROSWELL ALIEN-CON 1997

FEBRUARY 1, 1997 10 A.M. - 4 P.M.	ROSWELL CONVENTION CENTER	ADMISSION FOR THIS SPECIAL SHOW IS $5.00

PLUS: LIVE-SCREENING OF ALIEN AUTOPSY FOOTAGE!

**Paranormal Experts | Ghost Hunters | Alien Artifact Vendors
Cryptozoology Field Researchers | UFOlogists**

ALL THIS AND MORE! CALL FOR MORE INFORMATION

WITH SPECIAL GUESTS

RAY
ARTHUR
Host of paranormal
radio talk show,
LIGHTS IN SKY.

SIGNING
HIS NEW
BOOK
THE IMPENDING
Ray Arthur

BETTY
HILL
Alien abductee,
and inspiration for
THE INTERRUPTED
JOURNEY.

CREATED BY WINSTON GAMBRO

EDITED BY BEN GRANOFF

Lights in the Sky is the copyright of Winston Gambro, all rights reserved.
This is a work of fiction. Names, characters, businesses, places, events and incidents are either the products of
the writer's imagination or used in a fictitious manner. Any resemblance to actual persons, living or dead, or
actual events without satiric intent, is purely coincidental.

SPECIAL THANKS TO CLARK VON ALLEN,
KEVIN BIRTCHER, & SAM J. ROYALE

02-02-97 Recorded by: █████████

Ray Arthur: From the high desert and the great American
                  desert in the southwest, I bid you all
                  good morning or good afternoon, however
                  it may be. Welcome to Lights in the Sky.

                  As always, I'm your host, Ray Arthur. And
                  remember, we have no screening and only
                  have two rules: no bad words and you can
                  only call in once.

                  West of the Rockies, you're on the air.

Caller 264:   Hey Ray. First time, long time.

Ray Arthur: Callers, turn off your radio, please.

Caller 264   Oh. Sorry. So Anyway.

Caller 264   They did a follow up to the story you
                  covered, where those cows were found
                  mutilated. Do you remember that one?

Ray Arthur: Yes, I'm familiar.

Caller 264   In the bible, there's all this talk of cattle
                  sacrifice, do you think that could be related?

d by:

rom th
esert
od mo

FO UF
emembe
awhat
nly ca

ey Ray.

Caller 264   Oh

Ray Arthur: Farmers are sacrificing their cattle?

Caller 264:   No, well—

Caller 264:   Maybe?

Ray Arthur: Excellent point. A lot to think about.
                 Thank you for the call.

CALL ENDS

Ray Arthur: First time caller line, you're on the air.

Caller 265:   That last guy had it all wrong, he didn't
                 mention the crop circles!

Ray Arthur:

CALL ENDS

Ray

Cal   portal to another world!

I'VE BEEN TRYING TO CALL YOUR SHOW FOR MONTHS, HAVE YOU HEARD OF THE HALEY-BOPP COMET?
ROSWELL CONVENTION CENTER

IS THAT RELATED TO THE HALE-BOPP COMET?
THAT'S WHAT I MEANT. IT'S COMING SOON, AND I HEARD THERE'S A SPACESHIP TRAILING BEHIND IT.

YOU KNOW WHERE YOU HEARD THAT?
MY SHOW.
THE ASTRONOMER WHO PHOTOGRAPHED THE SHIP CALLED IN LAST MONTH.

BUT ANYWAY IT'S ALL A DISTRACTION FROM PLANET X, THIS GIANT--
AND WHO SHOULD I MAKE THE BOOK OUT TO?
THE IMPENDING
Roy Arthur
I've spent a lot of time in a tiny room by myself.

More than any person this side of a padded cell.
WHAT'S THE CRAZIEST CALL YOU'VE GOTTEN?
ARTHUR

IF HE REALLY TIME TRAVELED, WHY DID HE LAND ON EARTH? SINCE THE EARTH IS MOVING THROUGH SPACE, WOULDN'T HE HAVE APPEARED OFF-WORLD?
Unfortunately, I'm not alone...

JFK DIDN'T KILL HER! HE TRIED, BUT SHE FAKED HER DEATH, THEN SHE SHOT HIM! FROM THE GRASSY KNOLL!
...I'm surrounded by voices.
ARTHUR

BEFORE I BEGIN, YOU NEED AN IQ OF OVER 160 TO COMPREHEND MY THEORY.
BIGFOOT IS A DIMENSIONAL TRAVELER.
Voices like these.

AFTER PARSON'S RITUAL, WHAT HAPPENED? ROSWELL! HE PIERCED THE BARRIER!
ARTHUR
I wish they were just in my head.

They'd be easier to explain away.
ARTHUR

SORRY EVERYONE, MR. ARTHUR NEEDS TO TAKE A QUICK BREAK.
BUT HE KNOWS ME! I'M DAWN!
DAWN ESTRELLA!
I NEED TO TALK TO HIM, IT'S IMPORTANT!

Dawn Estrella!? The Dawn Estrella that calls into every show? That sends me a letter almost every week?
HEY KID, I'LL BE RIGHT BACK.

Every public figure has those fans.
FROZEN TRUTH
What REALLY happened at DYATLOV PASS
MAN PROPHECIES

The ones that take the parasocial relationship too far.
DAWN ESTRELLA
RAY ARTHUR

Better make it three cigarettes.

-KCK-

COUGH!-
COUGH!-

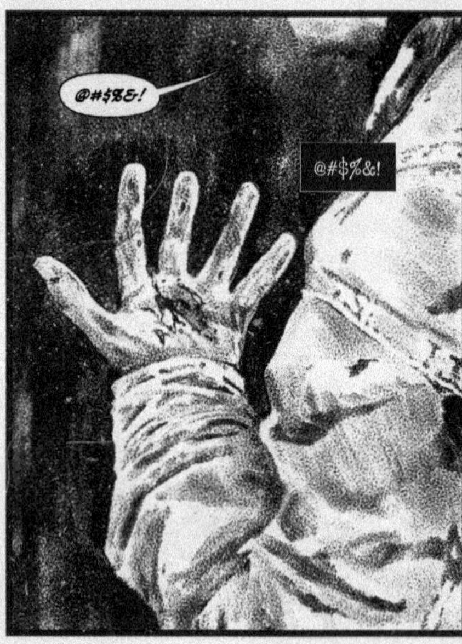

@#$&!
@#$%&!

VOYNICH MANUSCRIPT
FINALLY DECODED!
ARE W. ALONE
SASQUATCH CO
GONE SQUATCHIN
GONE SQUATCHIN
BIGFOOT FOOTPRINT CAST ONE LEFT!
How the hell did I end up like this?
Spending my final days fielding calls about bull$%^& like bigfoot and Area 51?

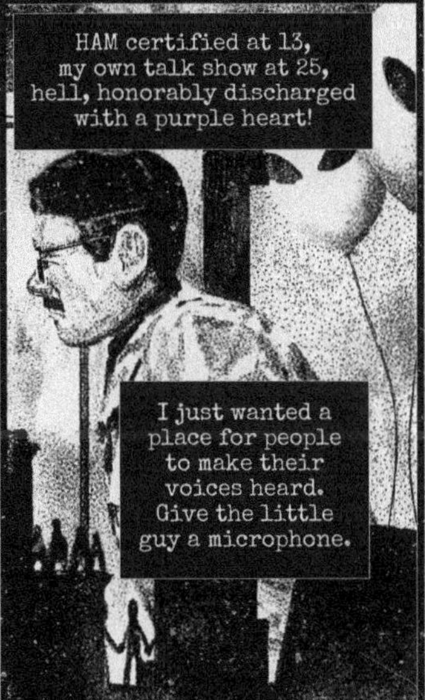

HAM certified at 13, my own talk show at 25, hell, honorably discharged with a purple heart!
I just wanted a place for people to make their voices heard. Give the little guy a microphone.

But the loudest voices are the craziest.
And the craziest get ratings.
And my producers like ratings.

Now I get paid to listen to nuts ramble about alien autopsies.

THE DEVIL HAS INFILTRATED THE WHITE HOUSE
There's no government conspiracy.

The government's not competent enough to cover anything up.
THE IMPENDING
MR. ARTHUR, I NEED TO TALK TO YOU.

AND I TRULY APPRECIATE YOU WAITING IN LINE TO DO SO.
AM I MAKING THIS OUT TO YOU?
COULD WE TALK PRIVATELY?
THE IMPENDING

THAT WOULDN'T BE VERY POLITE TO THE NICE PEOPLE WAITING BEHIND YOU.

MR. ARTHUR, PLEASE, IT'S ABOUT MY--
COME ON, MOVE IT!

RAY A

YOU CAN MAKE IT OUT TO ME.

MR. ARTHUR, BIG FAN
THE IMPENDING

APPRECIATE IT.
REGARDING YOUR BOOK, WHAT IF THE IMPENDING IS A RESULT OF MAN'S CRIMES AGAINST THE EARTH?

THAT'S AN INTERESTING THEORY.
DO YOU THINK IT'S TRUE?
THE IMPENDING
Ray Arthur
RAY

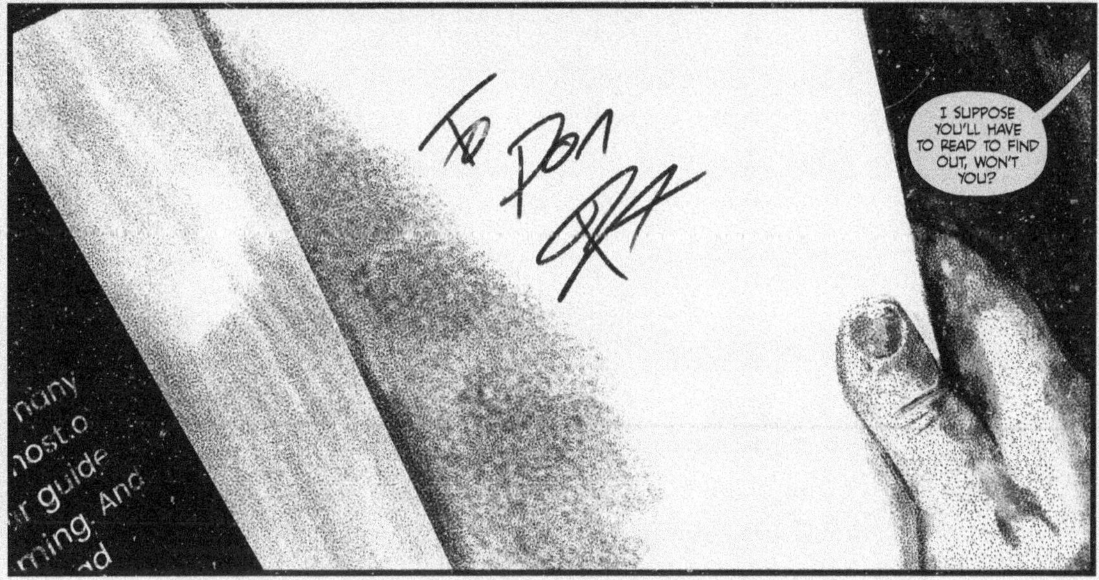

I SUPPOSE YOU'LL HAVE TO READ TO FIND OUT, WON'T YOU?
To Don
many
host.o
r guide
ming. And
d

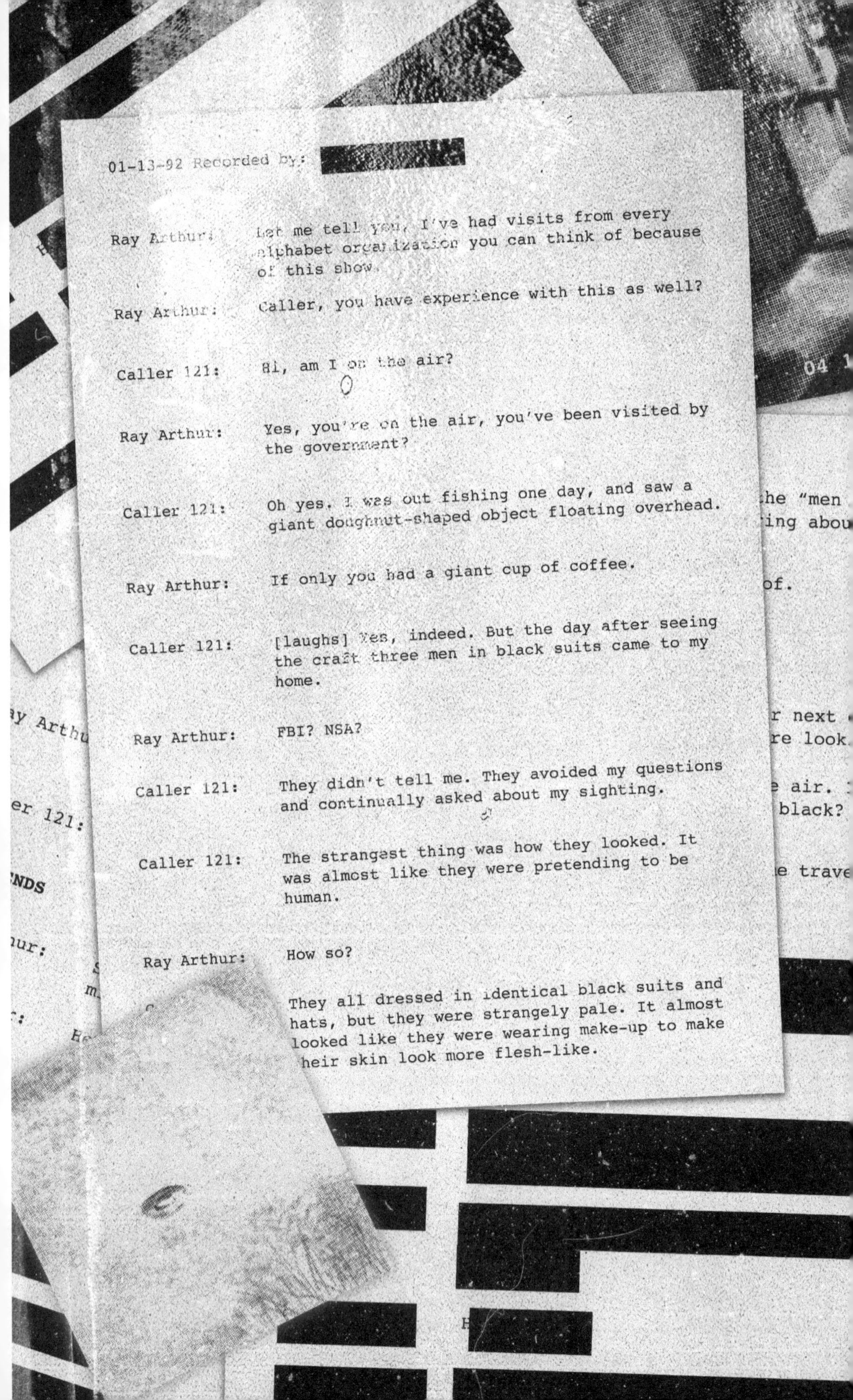

01-13-92 Recorded by:

Ray Arthur: Let me tell you, I've had visits from every
                alphabet organization you can think of because
                of this show.

Ray Arthur: Caller, you have experience with this as well?

Caller 121:   Hi, am I on the air?

Ray Arthur: Yes, you're on the air, you've been visited by
                the government?

Caller 121:   Oh yes. I was out fishing one day, and saw a
                giant doughnut-shaped object floating overhead.

Ray Arthur: If only you had a giant cup of coffee.

Caller 121:   [laughs] Yes, indeed. But the day after seeing
                the craft three men in black suits came to my
                home.

Ray Arthur: FBI? NSA?

Caller 121:   They didn't tell me. They avoided my questions
                and continually asked about my sighting.

Caller 121:   The strangest thing was how they looked. It
                was almost like they were pretending to be
                human.

Ray Arthur: How so?

                They all dressed in identical black suits and
                hats, but they were strangely pale. It almost
                looked like they were wearing make-up to make
                their skin look more flesh-like.

Ray Arthur: Oh no, that sounds like the "men
                 in black" we've been hearing about.

Caller 121:   That's what I was afraid of.

CALL ENDS

Ray Arthur: Scary, scary stuff. But our next caller
                 might have the answers we're looking for.

Ray Arthur: Hello caller, you're on the air. I
                 understand you're a man in black?

Caller 122:   Correct Ray, I'm also a time traveler.

LAR 1.19
DED 1.29
HAYES
HAYES
HAYES
I'M CHECKING THE STATUS OF FLIGHT 5885.

HOW DELAYED?
IT'S FINE
IF THIS YOUR
$5 &.
THANKS.

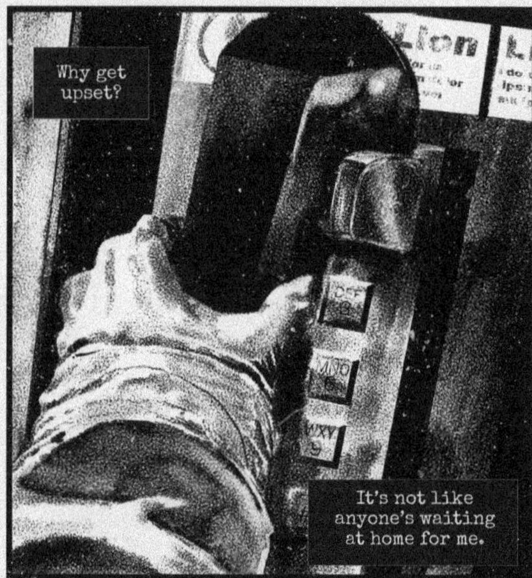
Lion
Why get upset?
It's not like anyone's waiting at home for me.

POLYBIUS
HAYES
Closest thing I have to family are the nuts that call into my show.
BUY 1 GET 1 FREE

{COUGH{
{COUGH{
And I wouldn't have been forced to meet them if it wasn't for this...

...inconvenience.
{COUGH{
{COUGH{
{HCK{

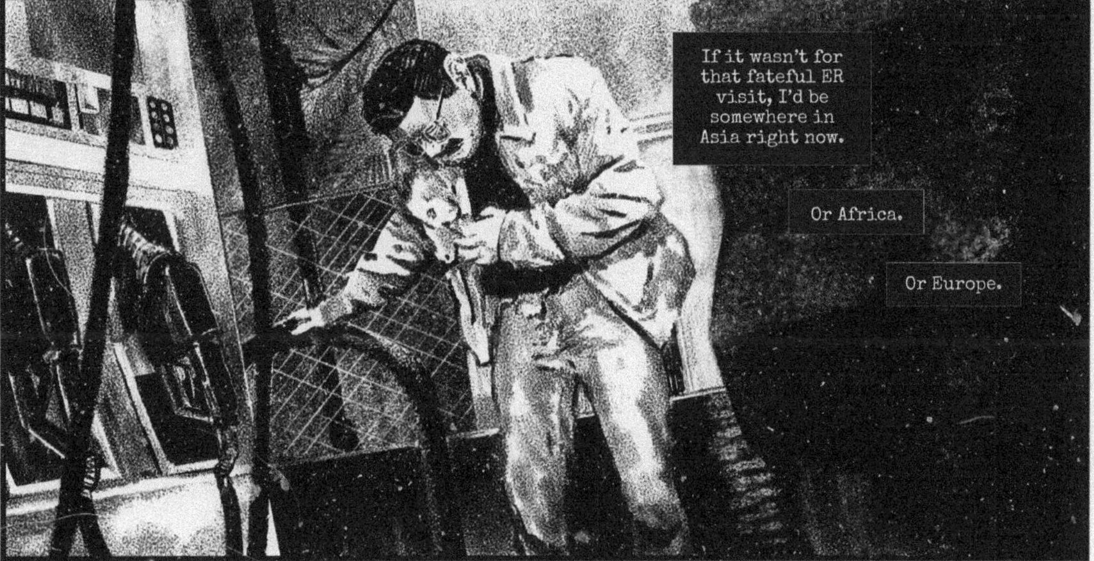

If it wasn't for that fateful ER visit, I'd be somewhere in Asia right now.
Or Africa.
Or Europe.

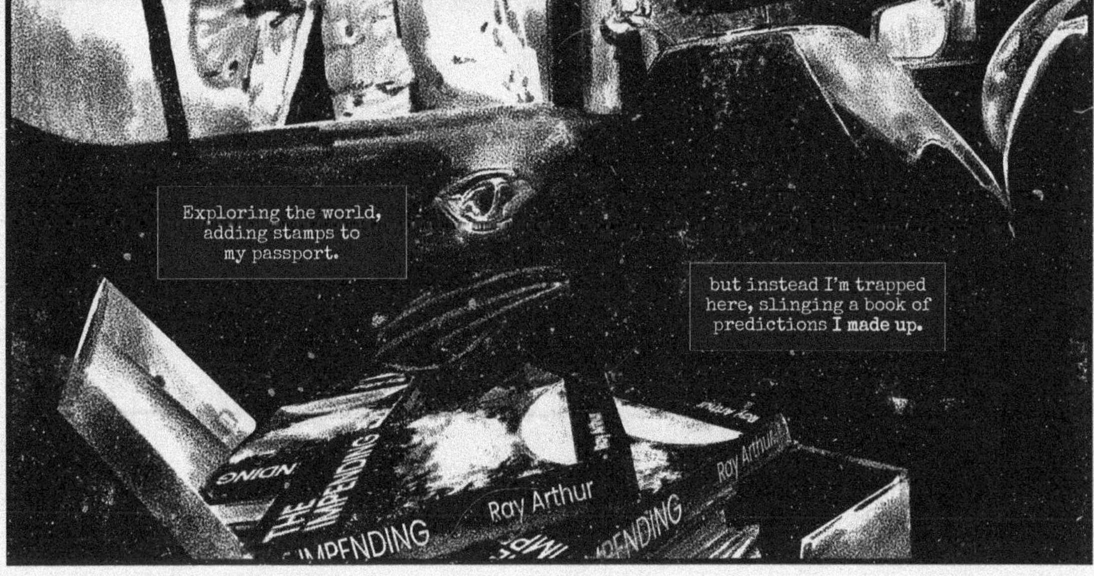

Exploring the world, adding stamps to my passport.
but instead I'm trapped here, slinging a book of predictions I made up.
THE IMPENDING
Ray Arthur

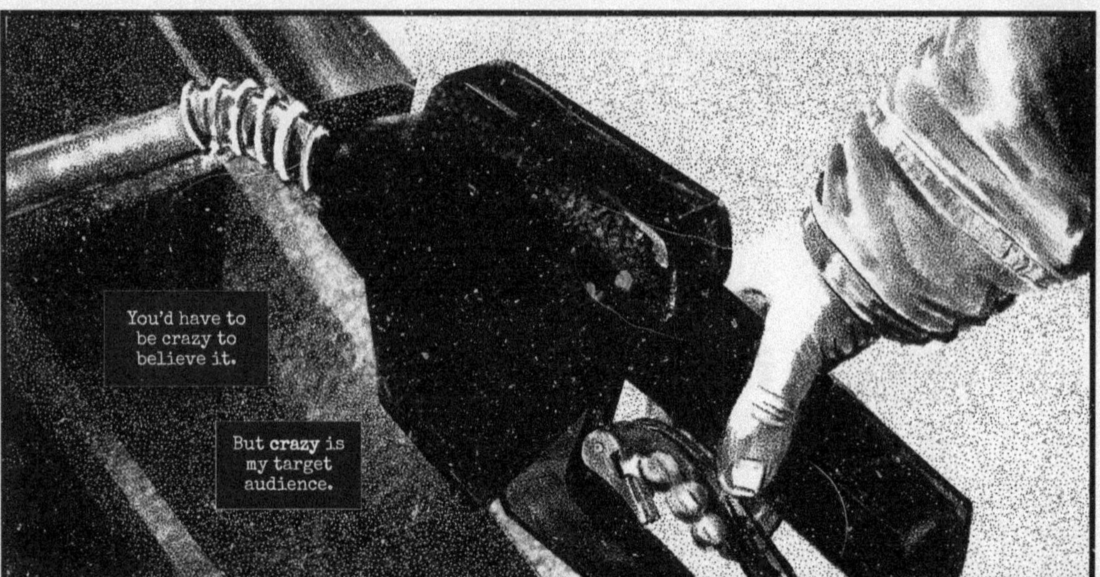

You'd have to be crazy to believe it.

But crazy is my target audience.

I avoided meeting my callers like the plague.

Until I realized how expensive my treatment would be.

And how much a new book would sell.

YOU'RE LISTENING TO TJ AND THE DONKEY PUNCH IN THE MORNING!
≈HEE-HAW!≈
HACKS.

≈COUGH≈
≈COUGH≈
MR. ARTHUR?

OH, DAWN, RIGHT?
THE SIGNING IS OVER FOR TODAY. YOU CAN TRY TO CATCH ME AT THE NEXT ONE.
I NEED TO TALK TO YOU.

4.26 Sale
3.752 Gallons
19 1.89

YOU GOT ME UNTIL THE TANK IS FULL.
YOU'RE THE ONLY ONE WHO CAN HELP ME. I NEED YOU TO COME WITH ME.
Uh-oh.

TICK.
4 55 Sal
4.215 Onl
TICK.
1.09
TICK.

I KNOW YOU'RE A BIG FAN.
SO YOU KNOW I ALWAYS HAVE A GUN ON ME.

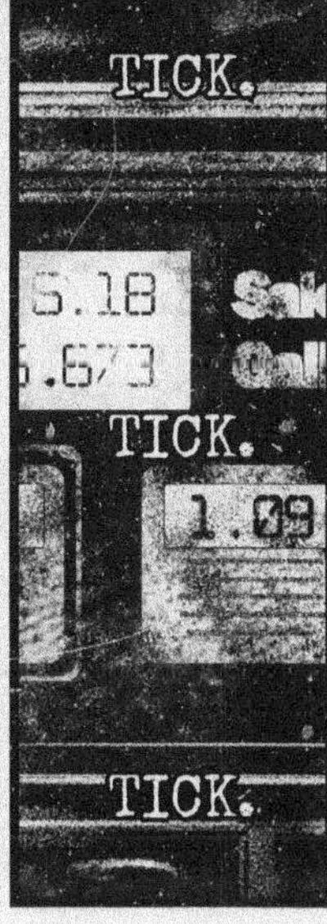

TICK.
5.18 Sal
6.673 Onl
TICK.
1.09
TICK.

IT'S ABOUT MY BABY!
THEY STOLE MY LUCY!
And here we go.

TICK.
6.86
6.532
Sale
Gall
19
1.09
TICK.

DAWN, CALM DOWN.
WE CAN CALL THE POLICE, THEY HANDLE THIS SORT OF THING.
Defuse.
Then hand her off.

TICK.
7.76
7.122
19
1.09
TICK.

NO!
THEY WON'T BELIEVE ME! NO ONE WILL!
ONLY YOU WILL!
It's not my first time dealing with a crazy, but they're not usually this intense.

TICK.
8.64
7.934
Sale
Gall
19
1.09
TICK.
TICK.

WHAT DO YOU MEAN BY ONLY ME?
ONLY YOU'LL BELIEVE ME BECAUSE YOU LISTEN TO PEOPLE LIKE ME!
YOU UNDERSTAND HIGH STRANGENESS!
Or loud.

TICK.
9.07
8.329
Sale
Gall
19
1.09
TICK.
TICK.

OH I DEFINITELY UNDERSTAND.
I'M CALLING THE POLICE RIGHT NOW, JUST CALM DOWN. THEY'LL GET YOU THE HELP YOU NEED.
MR. ARTHUR, PLEASE!
Distance yourself now.

TICK.
10.43
9.569
Sale
Gall
19
1.09
TICK.
TICK.

EXTRATERRESTRIALS TOOK HER!

10.90
10.000
Sale
Gall
19
1.09
DING!

HAYES
HAYES
...

YOUR CONSTANT CALLS AND LETTERS AREN'T ENOUGH?
NOW YOU DECIDE TO STALK ME WITH THIS INSANE STORY? IS THAT IT?
THEY TOOK LUCY! RIGHT OUT OF MY HANDS!

I KNOW IT SOUNDS CRAZY, THAT'S WHY I COULDN'T GO TO THE POLICE, OR THE FBI OR ANYONE!
THEY'D LOCK ME UP THINKING I DID SOMETHING TO HER!

YOU'RE THE ONLY ONE THAT COULD HELP ME. YOU KNOW MORE ABOUT THIS STUFF THAN ANYONE!
And because I know about it, I know it's all bull$%^&.

PLEASE.
...

YOU NEED HELP, BUT *NOT FROM ME.* YOU'RE COMPLETELY INSA--

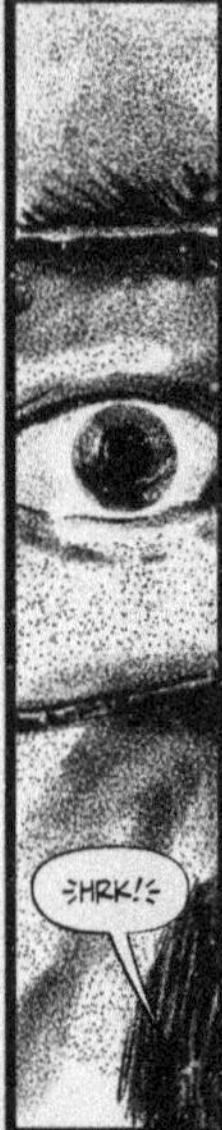

⊰HRK!⊱

⊰COUGH⊱
⊰COUGH⊱

ARE YOU OKAY?
⊰COUGH⊱
⊰COUGH⊱

⊰HK⊱
This is how my life ends?

Choking on my own pain, in a puddle of gasoline?
No wife, no kids. Just a maniac attempting to save me with amateur chest compressions.

This can't be it.

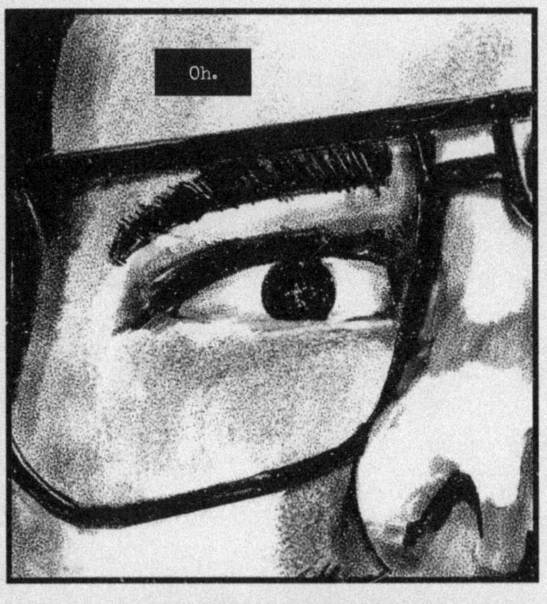
Oh.

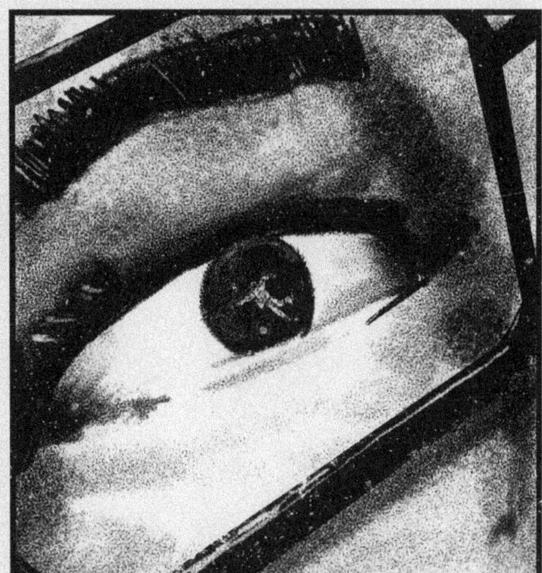

I guess it is.

This isn't that bad.

06-01-91 Recorded by: ████████████

Ray Arthur: Welcome back. If you're just joining us, tonight we're talking all about the Philadelphia Experiment. A 1943 government experiment in which they made the USS Eldridge disappear and the crew aboard was thrown throughout time and space.

Ray Arthur: First time caller line, you're on the air.

Caller 112:   Hello? Hello? Ray? Am I on?

Ray Arthur: Yes, caller, what's your name and where are you calling from?

Caller 112:   I'd like to stay anonymous. I was a sailor aboard the USS Eldridge when the experiment was conducted.

Ray Arthur: Really? Incredible. Can you describe your experience?

Caller 112:   We knew it was some sort of new science, but next thing I knew, the entire boat was in a different ocean! The harbor was completely gone!

Caller 112:   It was pure chaos as soon as we appeared into the new location, some men were missing but they got off easy.

Caller 112:   Some sailors were fused to the deck of the ship!

Ray Arthur: Dear god. They were melded into it?

Caller 112:   It was like they had been merged into the
               walls and floors. They were screaming. It was
               awful.

Caller 112:   My brother- he was a sailor as well. He
               disappeared that night.

Ray Arthur: Oh no. I'm so sorry for your loss.

Caller 112:   But he didn't die.

Ray Arthur: Oh?

Caller 112:   Like everyone, I thought he did too, but I got
               a knock on my door just a month ago.

Caller 112:   My brother was standing there. Looking not a
               day over 25. He had been thrown into our time!

What-

Oh.
I'm not dead.

Yet.
≶COUGH≶

YOU'RE AWAKE!

I SUPPOSE-- I--
DAWN? WHERE THE HELL AM I?

AFTER YOU PASSED OUT, I LOADED YOU INTO MY CAR. WE'RE ON THE WAY TO THE HOSPITAL.
OH. THANK YOU.

HOW LONG HAVE YOU BEEN SICK-
I DON'T WANT TO TALK ABOUT IT.

YOU CAN DROP ME OFF, I CAN GET A TAXI.
I need to get out of here.
There's no way this ends without me tied up in her basement.

DROP YOU OFF? THERE'S NOTHING AROUND FOR MILES!
Of course.
Why would there be?

THE FIRST REST STOP THEN. I'D HATE TO BE A BURDEN.
BURDEN? I NEED YOU!

YOU'RE THE ONLY ONE WHO MIGHT KNOW HOW TO TALK TO THEM.
THEM?

THE VENUSIANS. THE EXTRATERRESTRIALS THAT TOOK MY LUCY.
I'VE BEEN TALKING TO THEM FOR YEARS, SINCE I WAS A KID.
Doors locked. Probably can open them without her noticing but then what?

MY FAMILY WAS CAMPING IN THE DESERT.
IN THE MIDDLE OF THE NIGHT, I JUST FELT THIS TUG TO LEAVE MY TENT.
TO JUST WANDER AWAY.
Roll onto the dirt road and run? With this cough?

HAVE YOU EXPERIENCED MIDNIGHT IN THE DESERT?
IT'S MAGICAL. IT FEELS LIKE YOU'RE ALONE IN THE UNIVERSE. JUST YOU AND THE STARS.

AND THEN HE APPEARED.
THAT'S WHEN I MET VAL.

AND WHO IS VAL?

VAL IS A VENUSIAN, THE ONE THAT INITIATED ME INTO HIS CULTURE.

HE CHANGED EVERYTHING. MY WHOLE PERCEPTION OF THE UNIVERSE.
HOW MANY TIMES HAVE YOU INTERACTED WITH VAL?

INTERACTED?
THAT MAKES IT SOUND SO... CLINICAL.
VAL WAS MORE THAN JUST A DISTANT VISITOR. HE BECAME A FRIEND, A GUIDE TO THE COSMOS.

SO YOU SAW HIM A LOT.

HIS PEOPLE USE COMETS AND OTHER CELESTIAL EVENTS TO TRAVEL, SO HE WAS BOUND BY CHANCE.
HE WANTED TO SEE ME MORE, BUT HE COULD ONLY VISIT EVERY COUPLE OF YEARS.

And I'm sure she got plenty of pictures of him.
IN ALL OF THESE VISITS, WHAT DID YOU DO?
DID YOU SHOW HIM AROUND EARTH?

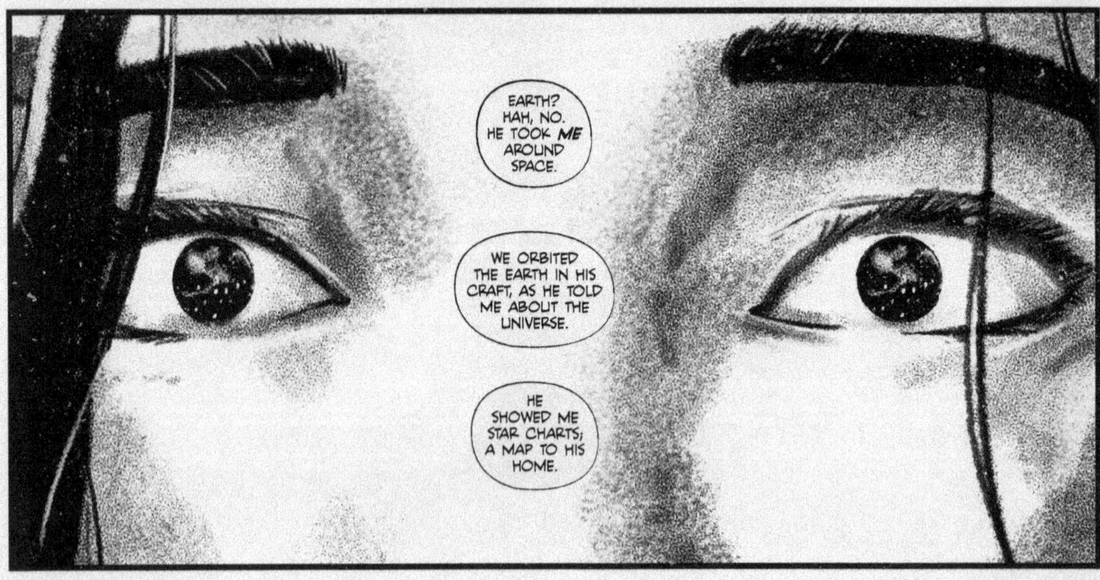

EARTH? HAH, NO. HE TOOK ME AROUND SPACE.
WE ORBITED THE EARTH IN HIS CRAFT, AS HE TOLD ME ABOUT THE UNIVERSE.
HE SHOWED ME STAR CHARTS; A MAP TO HIS HOME.

AND YOU MEET HIM IN THE SAME SPOT FROM WHEN YOU WERE YOUNGER?
THE CAMPSITE?

NOT FOR YEARS.
Convenient.
WHEN I CAME TO THE DESERT, HE MOVED THE MEETING SPOT TO A MILE FROM MY HOME.

O YOU KNOW THIS MAN?
ANY INFORMATION CA
910-232-16
NOW I DRIVE OUT TO THE MIDDLE OF THE DESERT.
AN ABANDONED BILLBOARD IS MY LANDMARK.

≒COUGH≒
DON'T TAKE THIS THE WRONG WAY
WHY YOU?

...
I DON'T KNOW.

ISN'T IT LIKE ANY SORT OF UNIQUE EXPERIENCE?
WHY IS YOUR SHOW THE ONLY ONE THAT CARES ABOUT PEOPLE LIKE ME?
WHY YOU?

LIKE EVERY SUCCESS IN THE WORLD:
HARD WORK AND CHANCE.
≶COUGH≶

AND BY CHANCE, I DON'T MEAN FATE.
FATE IS THE LAZY MAN'S EXPLANATION FOR SUCCEEDING.

AFTER WHAT I SAW IN VIETNAM...

I HAD TO CLEAR MY HEAD. MAKE SENSE OF THE WORLD. TRAVELED AS MUCH AS I COULD. TALKED TO EVERYONE. TRIED TO FIND SOME ANSWERS.
VIETNAM? YOU DON'T TALK ABOUT THAT ON THE SHOW.

NO, I DON'T.

I LIVED A LOT OF LIVES.

LEARNED A LOT TOO.

BUT THOSE ANSWERS I WAS LOOKING FOR?

DIDN'T FIND THEM.
CAME BACK AND THOUGHT IF I LISTENED TO OTHERS, MAYBE THEY'D HAVE THE ANSWERS I NEEDED.
ALL THEY HAD WAS MORE QUESTIONS.
≈COUGH≈

SO WHY DO THE ALIEN ABDUCTEES AND BIGFOOT HUNTERS CALL INTO MY SHOW?
HARD WORK AND CHANCE.

HARD WORK TO GET WHERE I AM, CHANCE THAT IT BECAME THE CIRCUS IT IS TODAY.

FAST FORWARD A DECADE OR TWO, AND NOW I'M IN A CAR WITH A WOMAN THAT'S BEST FRIENDS WITH A VENUSIAN.

VENUSIAN IS LIMITING.
...DO YOU REMEMBER WHEN YOU HAD THAT DOCTOR ON WHO TALKED ABOUT THE HULDUFÓLK?

THE ICELANDIC GNOMES? HARD TO FORGET.
THEY WEREN'T GNOMES, THEY WERE PARALLEL BEINGS. SOMETHING WE COULDN'T COMPREHEND; THAT OUR MINDS WARPED INTO SOMETHING FAMILIAR.
Oh that clarifies it.
BUT THEY-- THEY WANTED KNOWLEDGE.
THEY WOULD TRADE GIFTS OR POWER FOR INFORMATION ABOUT OUR WORLD?

KNOWLEDGE, HUH?
IT REMINDED ME OF VAL.

HE WANTED- WANTS TO KNOW EVERYTHING ABOUT US.
AND IN RETURN HE GAVE ME WHAT I WANTED MOST.

AND IT'S SUPPOSED TO MAKE ME FEEL MORE CONFIDENT THAT YOUR ALIEN PAL MIGHT BE AN INTERDIMENSIONAL GNOME?
THE GREAT SANDOWN CIRCUS!

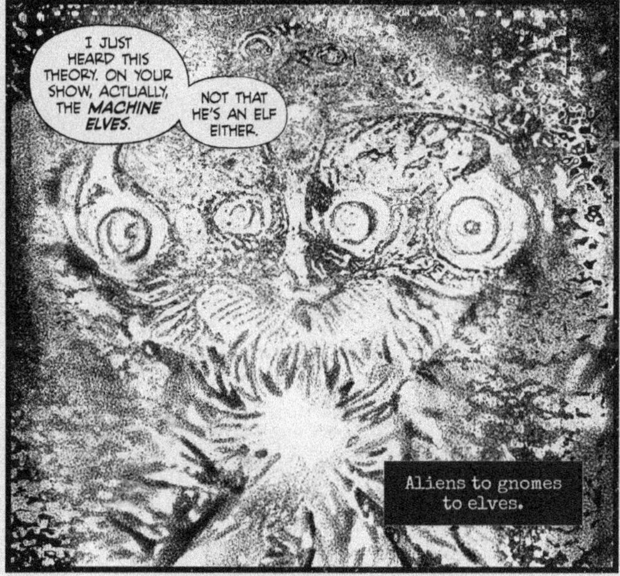

Aliens to gnomes to elves.

Like a gorilla man or a dinosaur in a Scottish lake.

SO YOU SOLVE ALL THE QUESTIONS WITH ONE ANSWER.

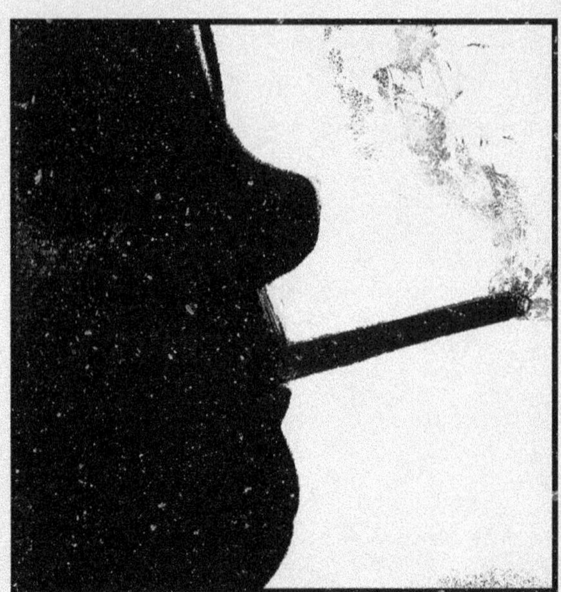

DAWN, WE'RE NOT GOING TO THE HOSPITAL, ARE WE?

MR. ARTHUR, I'M SORRY I LIED.

BUT WE'RE HERE NOW.

09-27-95 Recorded by: ▮▮▮▮▮▮▮▮▮▮

Ray Arthur: By far our most requested topic: Y2K. I swear
               every day I get more letters than the day
               before begging me to discuss what's going to
               happen. I thought the best solution would be
               to open up the phone lines and let the
               experts call in.

Ray Arthur: West of the Rockies, you're on the air.

Caller 103:   Ray? Oh thank god I made it on.

Ray Arthur: And we're thrilled as well. Did you have
               thoughts on the Y2K calamity approaching?

Caller 103:   Yes, yes, I'm a computer programmer and the
               threats coming are... in a word: terrifying.

Ray Arthur: What sort of threats?

Caller 103:   Every computer in the world failing
               simultaneously. Losing power, airplanes
               falling out of the sky! Hell, the nuclear
               arsenal could implode!

Ray Arthur: Watch the language, please.

Caller 103:   Uh, yes of course. Sorry Ray. But you can't
               even imagine how many things have a computer
               in them now, even things you wouldn't think
               about, like medical equipment.

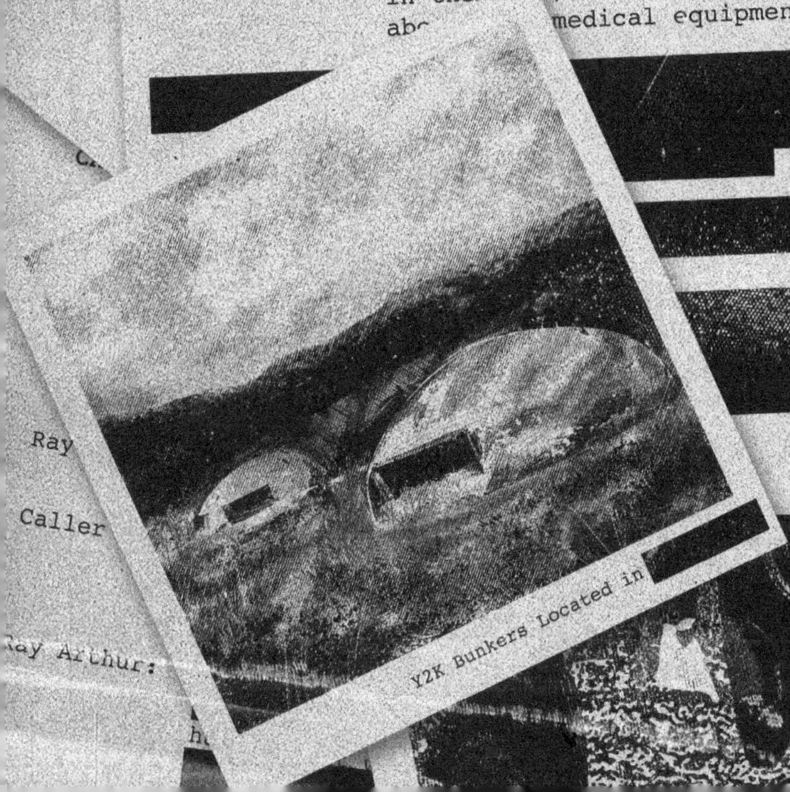

09-27-95 Recorded by: ▮▮▮▮▮▮▮▮

Caller 103:   Thanks, Ray.

CALL ENDS

Ray Arthur: Caller, you're on the air.

Caller 104:   Hey Ray, first time, long time. I'm a prison
              guard and I just have to get out of here
              before 2000 hits.

Ray Arthur: And why is that?

Caller 104:   This whole place is run by computers! If they
              go down, what's to stop every cell door from
              opening? It's going to be a massacre.

Ray Arthur: Callers, I know this is all very scary stuff,
              and I can't make any promises what will
              happen. But what I can promise is Lights in
              the Sky will be broadcasting on New Years Eve
              1999.

Ray Arthur: And whatever happens, we'll experience it
              together.

Idea for next book: An insane fan kidnaps a celebrity author, she tortures him and—

Misery.
IF YOU'RE LOOKING FOR YOUR GUN, I THREW IT OUT AT THE GAS STATION.

Misery already exists.

I'm just living it.

Play along. Go into interview-mode until there's a chance of escape.
HOW DID VAL TAKE YOUR CHILD?
HE TALKS TO ME THROUGH MY PC.
Maybe she'll fall asleep and I can take her keys.
Or the police will stop by for a wellness check.
Or I'll die chained to her radiator.

THAT'S HOW HE'S COMMUNICATED WITH ME FOR YEARS.

HE HADN'T MET LUCY YET, AND HE TOLD ME TO BRING HER INTO THE DESERT- TO THE BILLBOARD.
IS MAN?

I WAS STANDING IN THE DESERT, WAITING FOR HIM, HOLDING LUCY.
THEN SUDDENLY EVERYTHING WENT WHITE.

IT WAS SO SCARY, HE'D NEVER DONE THAT TO ME BEFORE.
SUDDENLY EVERYTHING WAS BACK TO NORMAL, EXCEPT...

LUCY.

LUCY WAS GONE.

She definitely believes it happened.

Not sure if that's more or less concerning.

WHY DO YOU LIVE OUT HERE?
WHY IN THE MIDDLE OF NOWHERE?

IT WAS VAL'S IDEA.
NO ONE AROUND TO SEE HIM.

So this is what's on the other end of the line.
IT'S— IT'S BEEN HARD TO DO ANYTHING SINCE THEN.
I'M SORRY ABOUT THE MESS.
Desperation and chaos.
HOW LONG AGO WAS THE ABDUCTION?

A WEEK.

I'VE SPENT HOURS EVERYDAY SINCE TRYING TO CONTACT VAL.
JUST SITTING AT MY COMPUTER, WAITING FOR HIM TO RESPOND.

NO RESPONSE?
NO.
AND THIS ISN'T LIKE VAL, HE NEVER WOULD JUST USE ME LIKE THIS.

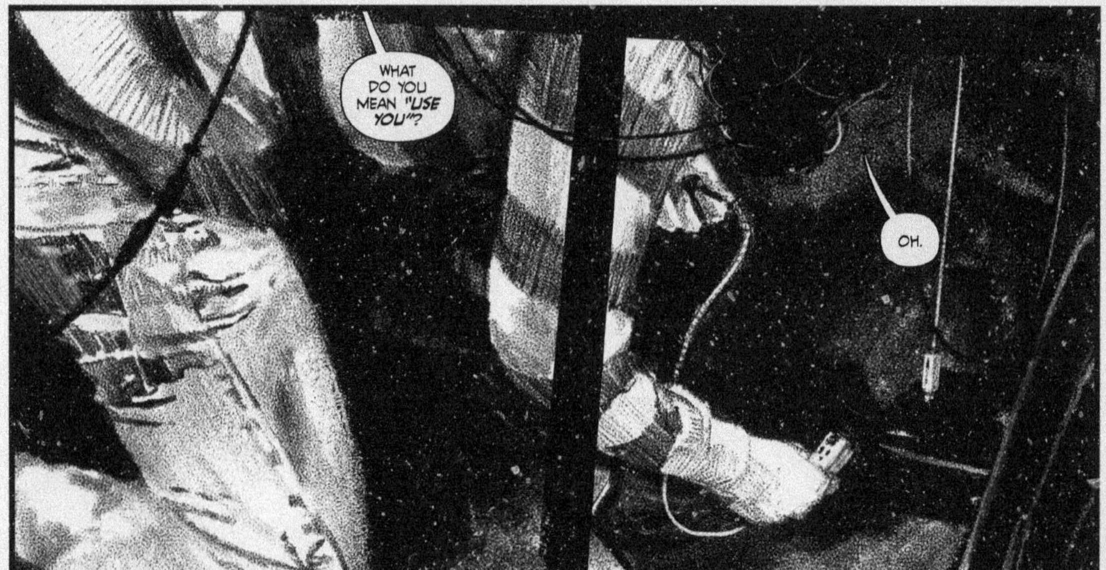

WHAT DO YOU MEAN "USE YOU"?
OH.

Take cover, a bomb is coming.
OH?

VAL IS LUCY'S FATHER.

SORRY, THOUGHT I MENTIONED THAT.

NO, I WOULD HAVE REMEMBERED THAT.
I'm not getting out of here alive.

If this baby ever existed, which it probably didn't—CPS probably took it after seeing this dump.

If I don't think of something, I'll die here.
What the hell am I going to do?

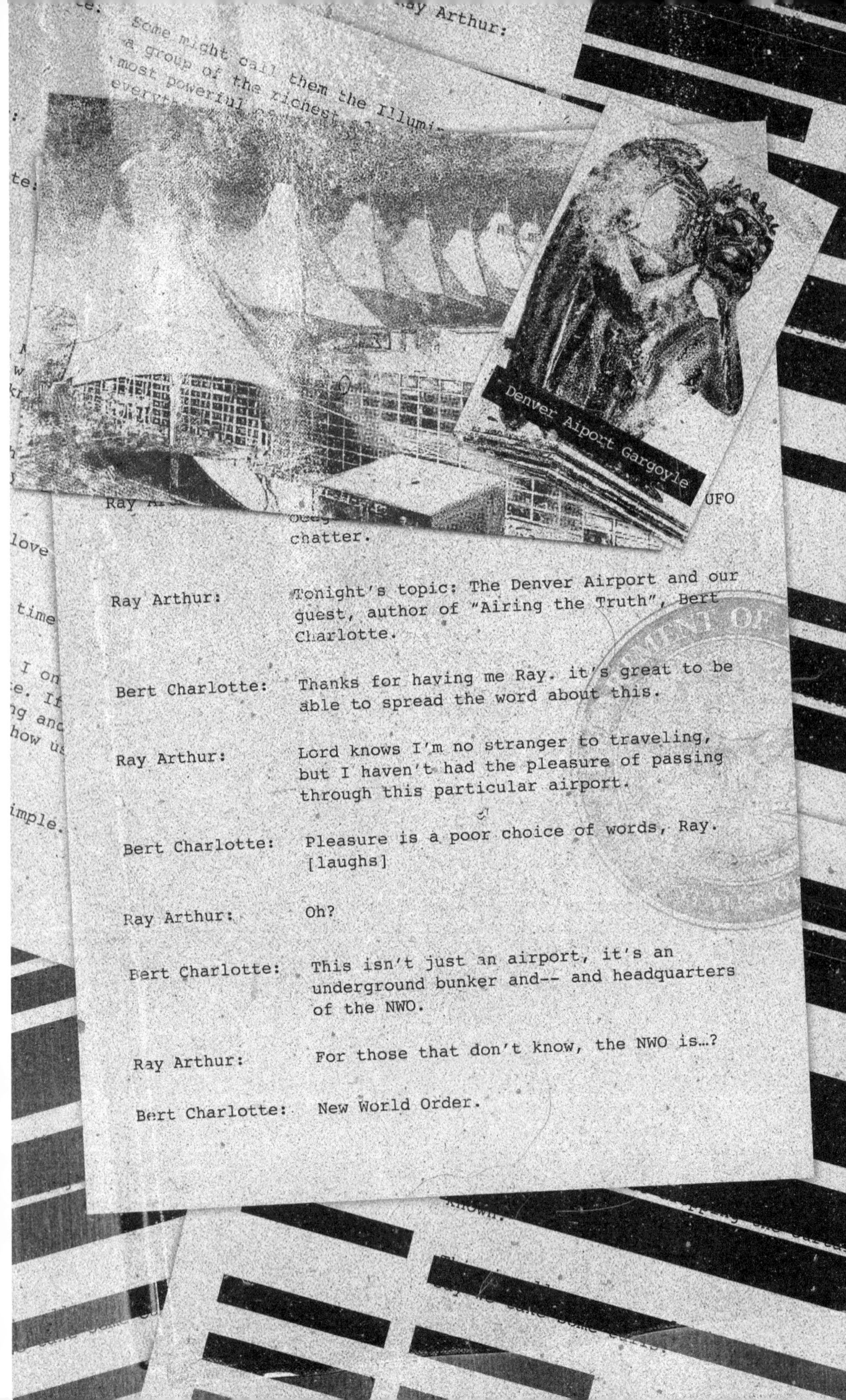

Ray Arthur: Tonight's topic: The Denver Airport and our
                     guest, author of "Airing the Truth", Bert
                     Charlotte.

Bert Charlotte: Thanks for having me Ray. it's great to be
                     able to spread the word about this.

Ray Arthur: Lord knows I'm no stranger to traveling,
                     but I haven't had the pleasure of passing
                     through this particular airport.

Bert Charlotte: Pleasure is a poor choice of words, Ray.
                     [laughs]

Ray Arthur: Oh?

Bert Charlotte: This isn't just an airport, it's an
                     underground bunker and-- and headquarters
                     of the NWO.

Ray Arthur: For those that don't know, the NWO is…?

Bert Charlotte: New World Order.

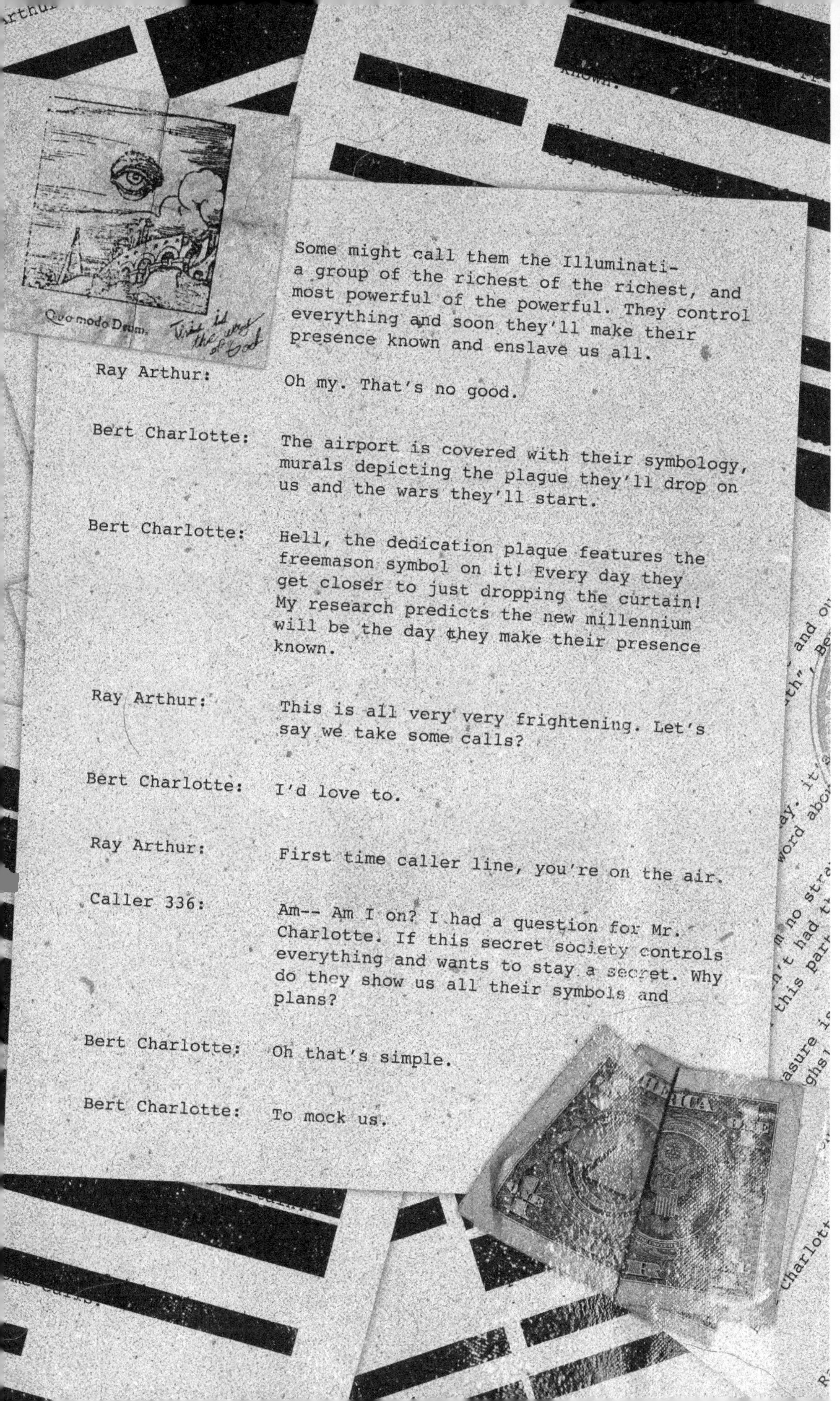

Some might call them the Illuminati-
a group of the richest of the richest, and
most powerful of the powerful. They control
everything and soon they'll make their
presence known and enslave us all.

Ray Arthur:

Oh my. That's no good.

Bert Charlotte:

The airport is covered with their symbology,
murals depicting the plague they'll drop on
us and the wars they'll start.

Bert Charlotte:

Hell, the dedication plaque features the
freemason symbol on it! Every day they
get closer to just dropping the curtain!
My research predicts the new millennium
will be the day they make their presence
known.

Ray Arthur:

This is all very very frightening. Let's
say we take some calls?

Bert Charlotte:

I'd love to.

Ray Arthur:

First time caller line, you're on the air.

Caller 336:

Am-- Am I on? I had a question for Mr.
Charlotte. If this secret society controls
everything and wants to stay a secret. Why
do they show us all their symbols and
plans?

Bert Charlotte:

Oh that's simple.

Bert Charlotte:

To mock us.

THE DISH ISN'T WORKING.

THE BIG ONE? YOU KNOW HOW TO FIX IT?
I USED TO BE A RADIO ENGINEER.

USED TO?
I- THINGS GOT HARD AT WORK, I HAD TO LEAVE.
Probably told her boss she was dating a Venusian.

I'LL GET IT FUNCTIONING AND BE RIGHT BACK.

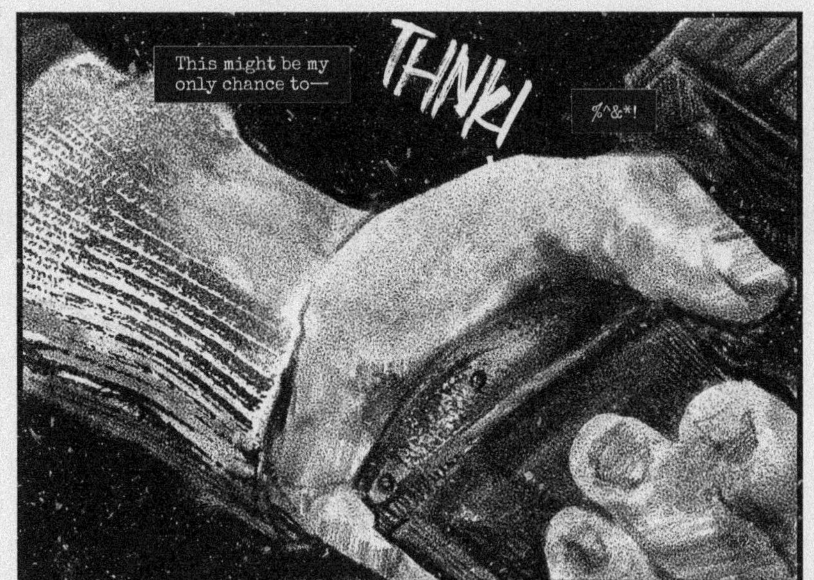
This might be my only chance to—
THNK!
%^&*!

:COUGH:
:COUGH:

MR. ARTHUR?
WERE—WERE YOU TRYING TO CLIMB OUT THE WINDOW?

DAWN, YOU NEED TO LET ME GO.
WHAT ARE YOU TALKING ABOUT!?
YOU HAVEN'T EVEN TALKED TO VAL!

DAWN, THIS STUFF ISN'T REAL.
YOU NEED HELP.

NO! NO! NOT YOU! YOU WERE MY ONLY CHANCE!
THE ONLY ONE WHO WOULD LISTEN!
THE MORE YOU LOOK INTO THIS STUFF, THE LESS REAL IT IS.

HAVE YOU THOUGHT OF HOW UFO TECHNOLOGY ADVANCES WITH OURS?
WHY AREN'T THERE CAVE DRAWINGS OF FLYING SAUCERS?

HELL, BACK IN THE 1800S THERE WAS A SIGHTING OF MEN PEDALING AN AIRSHIP.
BECAUSE THOSE POWDER-WIGS COULDN'T COMPREHEND AN ELECTRIC FLYING MACHINE!

BUT SO MANY PEOPLE HAVE SEEN THESE THINGS, THE BATTLE OF LOS ANGELES—

WAR-TIME NERVES AND A WEATHER BALLOON.

THE HOPKINSVILLE GOBLINS WERE—

DRUNK HILLBILLIES, PROBABLY HIGH ON LSD FROM MK-ULTRA.

ROSWELL—

THAT WAS A MILITARY DEVICE BUILT TO SPY ON THE SOVIETS.

YOU KNOW THE PATTERSON—GIMLIN BIGFOOT TAPE?

EVERYONE THINKS THEY WERE JUST SOME NATURE DOCUMENTARIANS THAT GOT LUCKY.
THAT CAUGHT SOME MONSTER STROLLING BY. THAT'S NOT THE CASE.

THEY WERE IN THE WOODS THAT DAY LOOKING FOR BIGFOOT.

SOMEHOW THAT FACTOID IS ALWAYS LEFT OUT. IT WASN'T SOME FREAK ENCOUNTER OR CATCH OF A LIFETIME.
IT WAS A COUPLE OF CHARLATANS AND A GORILLA SUIT.

THE MORE YOU LOOK INTO THIS STUFF, THE LESS REAL IT GETS.
IT'S ALL LIES AND GORILLA SUITS.
≥COUGH≥

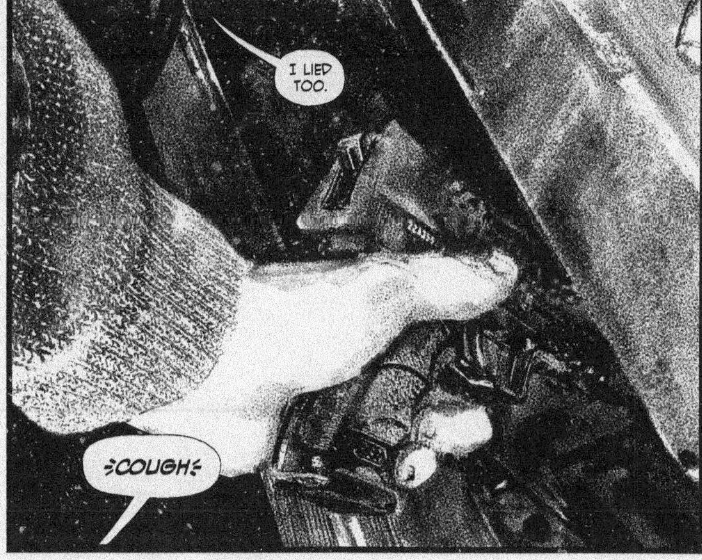

I LIED TOO.
≥COUGH≥

I DIDN'T THROW THE GUN OUT AT THE GAS STATION.
I NEED YOU TO BELIEVE ME.

So logical thinking was wrong.
$&`*! DAWN, PUT THAT DOWN. IT'S NOT A TOY.

YOU MAKE IT SOUND LIKE ALL YOUR LISTENERS ARE CRAZY!
I'M NOT CRAZY.

DAWN, HOLDING ME AT GUNPOINT ISN'T HELPING YOU LOOK SANE.

HOW CAN YOU BE LIKE THIS? AFTER ALL THE EVIDENCE— ALL THE CALLS!
DO YOU REALLY THINK EVERYONE IS LYING TO YOU?
I WANTED TO BELIEVE.

YOU HAVE NO IDEA HOW MANY PSYCHIC PREDICTIONS I'VE HEARD, HOW MANY OVERLAPPING GOVERNMENT CONSPIRACIES I'VE BEEN WARNED ABOUT.

I WROTE AN ENTIRE BOOK OF MY PREDICTIONS FOR THE FUTURE.
YOU KNOW WHY?
I DON'T HAVE SOME THIRD EYE OR EXTRASENSORY ABILITY.

BECAUSE I NEEDED MONEY.

THE FILES OF WHY?
AJ GENTILE
MISSING TIME
MALACETIC ATLAS
BUDD HOPKINS
Incredible Visitations at Copley Wood
THE SIRIUS MYSTERY
ROBERT K.G. TEMPLE
Chariots of the Gods?
ERICH VON DÄNIKEN
THE WALTON EXPERIENCE
Unexplained.
PHILADELPHIA EXPERIMENT: PROJECT INVISIBILITY
Richard MacLean Smith
Encounters
Communion
Whitley Strieber
Tales from the Void
AARON MARKNEY
Walter Flannagan
IF ANY OF THIS WAS REAL, WOULDN'T WE HAVE EVIDENCE BY NOW?
WOULDN'T THERE BE SOME SORT OF PROOF, NOT JUST BLIND FAITH?

YOU WANT PROOF? I HAVE PROOF!

I UNDERSTAND.
I'D LIKE TO SEE IT.
I WANT TO BELIEVE
Distract.

MY COMPUTER. I WAS GETTING IT TURNED ON TO SHOW YOU.
THIS IS HOW I TALK TO VAL.

SEE?

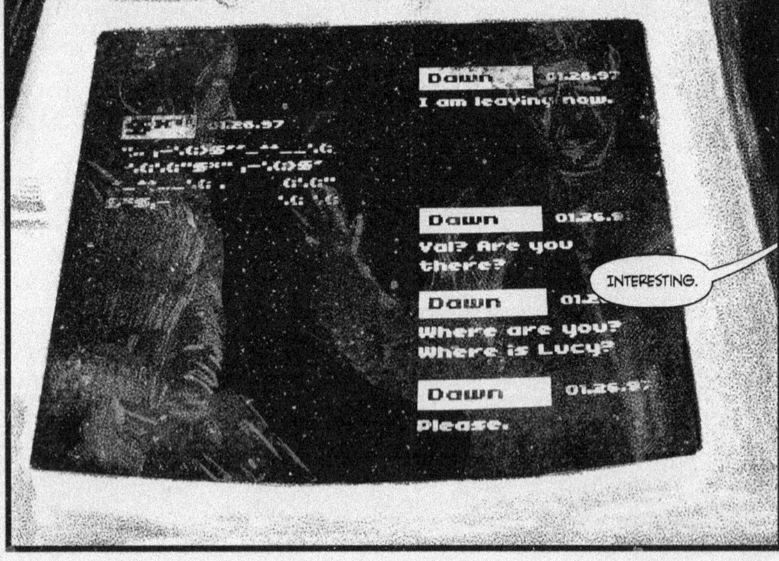

Dawn   01.26.97
I am leaving now.

01.26.97

Dawn   01.26.9
Val? Are you there?

Dawn   01.2
Where are you? Where is Lucy?

Dawn   01.26.9
Please.

INTERESTING.

SEE? THAT'S VAL TALKING TO ME!
HOW DO YOU UNDERSTAND THIS LANGUAGE?
It does seem like she's talking to someone.

VAL TAUGHT ME ENOUGH.
IT'S TOO COMPLICATED FOR A HUMAN TO FULLY UNDERSTAND THE LANGUAGE, BUT I CAN TELL WHEN HE'S VISITING.

AND I KNOW HE STOPPED REPLYING.
Roleplaying gone wrong? Maybe she met a guy online into this alien %&*$ and she scared him off.

Either way, there has to be someone on the other end of this.
THIS IS FASCINATING. JUST FASCINATING STUFF.

DAWN, I'M SORRY FOR NOT BELIEVING YOU.

THANK YOU.

VAL HAD A SPECIAL INTEREST IN THIS BOOK.
CLK
CLK
CLK
CLK
CLK

HE SAID IT WASN'T ACCURATE BUT--
CLK
CLK
CLK

WHAT ARE YOU TYPING?
The Truth comes from Venus!

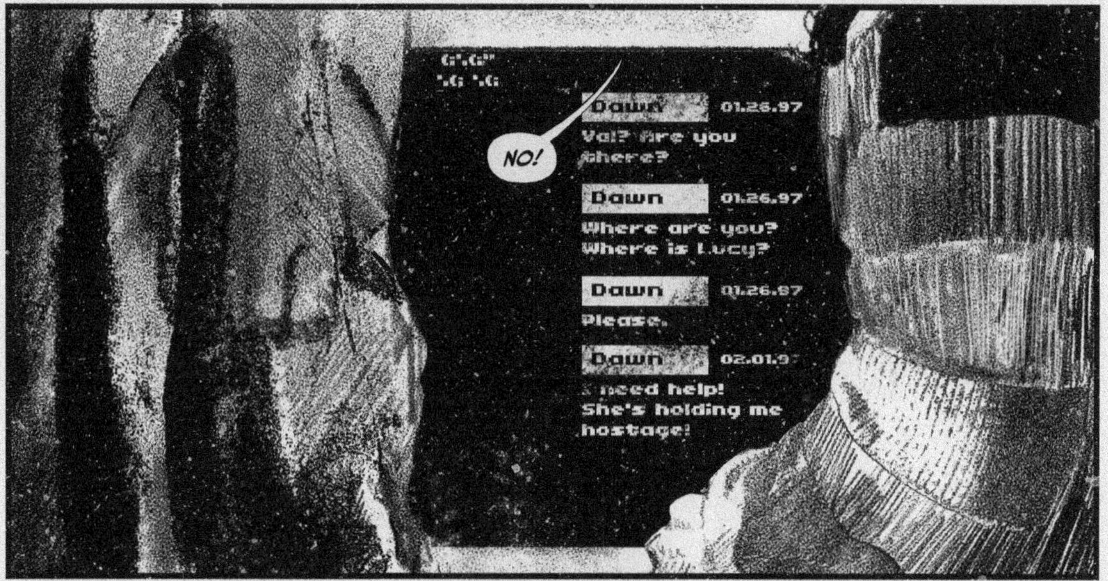

Dawn   01.26.97
Val? Are you there?
Dawn   01.26.97
Where are you? Where is Lucy?
Dawn   01.26.87
Please.
Dawn   02.01.9
I need help! She's holding me hostage!
NO!

WHY WOULD YOU DO THAT!?

VAL WILL THINK-

For some reason, I keep remembering Operation Wandering Soul.
It was a psychological warfare effort to scare the Viet Cong into surrender.
Didn't work.

I was a radio operator; part of the grunts that put it together.
Tried to scare the Viet Cong into deserting. Telling them if they didn't, they would die and haunt the Earth forever.

We made ghost sounds and blasted them into the jungle.

Problem was, the minute you start blasting spooky sounds into the darkness, they would start shooting back.

The last time I saw the stars like this, I was bleeding out in a swamp.

What did she say?

It feels like years ago at this point.

HAVE YOU EXPERIENCED MIDNIGHT IN THE DESERT?
IT'S MAGICAL. IT FEELS LIKE YOU'RE ALONE IN THE UNIVERSE. JUST YOU AND THE STARS.

I'm starting to understand what she means.

AGK!

I have a new pitch for the book.

How well do survival stories sell?

One of those where the guy gets stranded in the jungle and has to kill a tiger.

Never saw the appeal personally.

You know he survives.

MR. ARTHUR PLEASE, WE CAN TALK ABOUT THIS.

DEEP DOWN YOU KNOW. YOU KNOW I'M NOT CRAZY.
AND YOU KNOW WE CAN'T BE THE ONLY LIFE IN THE UNIVERSE.

LOOK UP AND TELL ME WE'RE ALONE.

JUST BECAUSE I DON'T BELIEVE IN LITTLE GRAY MEN DOESN'T MEAN WE'RE THE ONLY LIFE IN THE UNIVERSE.

BUT THE STUFF YOU'RE TALKING ABOUT...
IT'S—

AHH!
$^&*!
WHAT IS THIS?!
≶COUGH≶

NO!
NOT NOW!

VAL! NOT—
≶COUGH≶
≶COUGH≶
WHAT ARE YOU DOING?!

≶COUGH≶
≶COUGH≶
VAL!?
≶COUGH≶

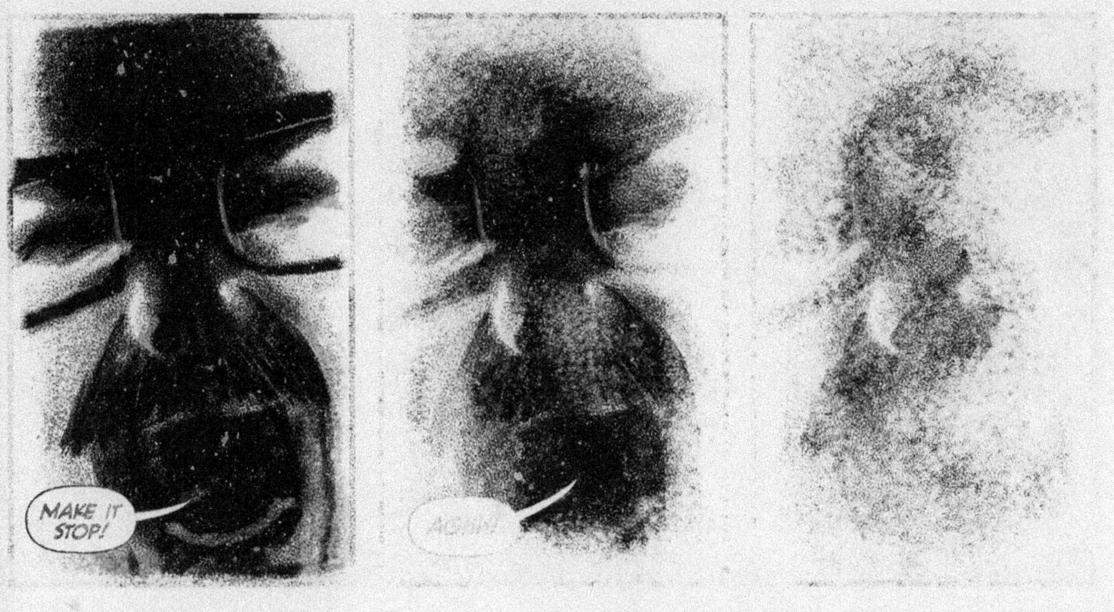

MAKE IT
STOP!
AGAIN!

≶COUGH≶

WHAT WAS
THAT?

DAWN?
≶COUGH≶

DAWN!
≶COUGH≶
YOU WERE
TELLING—
≶COUGH≶

YOU—
≶COUGH≶

≶COUGH≶
≶COUGH≶
≶COUGH≶

≶COUGH≶
≶HUFF≶

≶HUFF≶
≶HUFF≶
≶HU—

≶COUGH≶

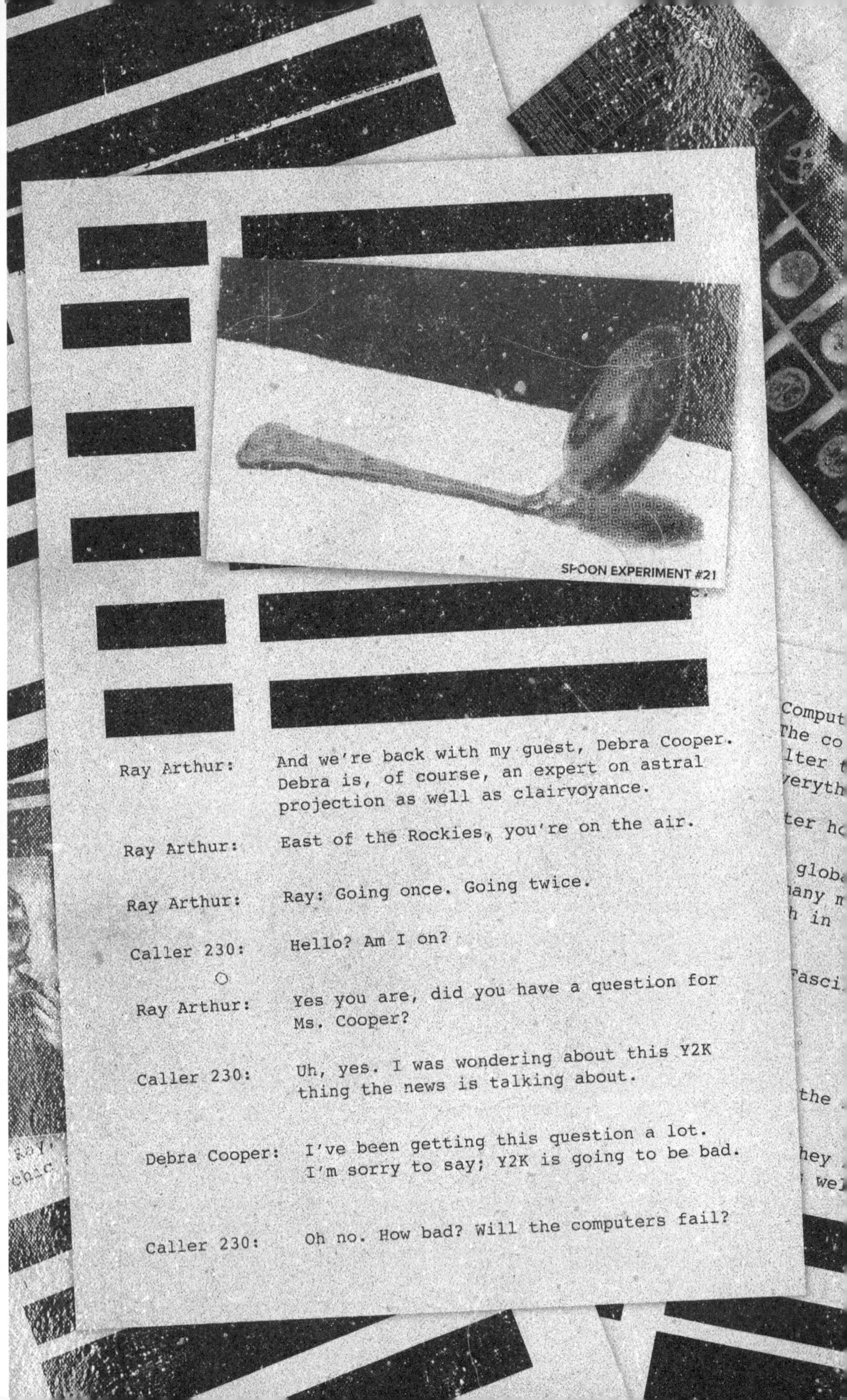

Ray Arthur: And we're back with my guest, Debra Cooper.
                 Debra is, of course, an expert on astral
                 projection as well as clairvoyance.

Ray Arthur: East of the Rockies, you're on the air.

Ray Arthur: Ray: Going once. Going twice.

Caller 230:   Hello? Am I on?

Ray Arthur: Yes you are, did you have a question for
                 Ms. Cooper?

Caller 230:   Uh, yes. I was wondering about this Y2K
                 thing the news is talking about.

Debra Cooper: I've been getting this question a lot.
                 I'm sorry to say; Y2K is going to be bad.

Caller 230:   Oh no. How bad? Will the computers fail?

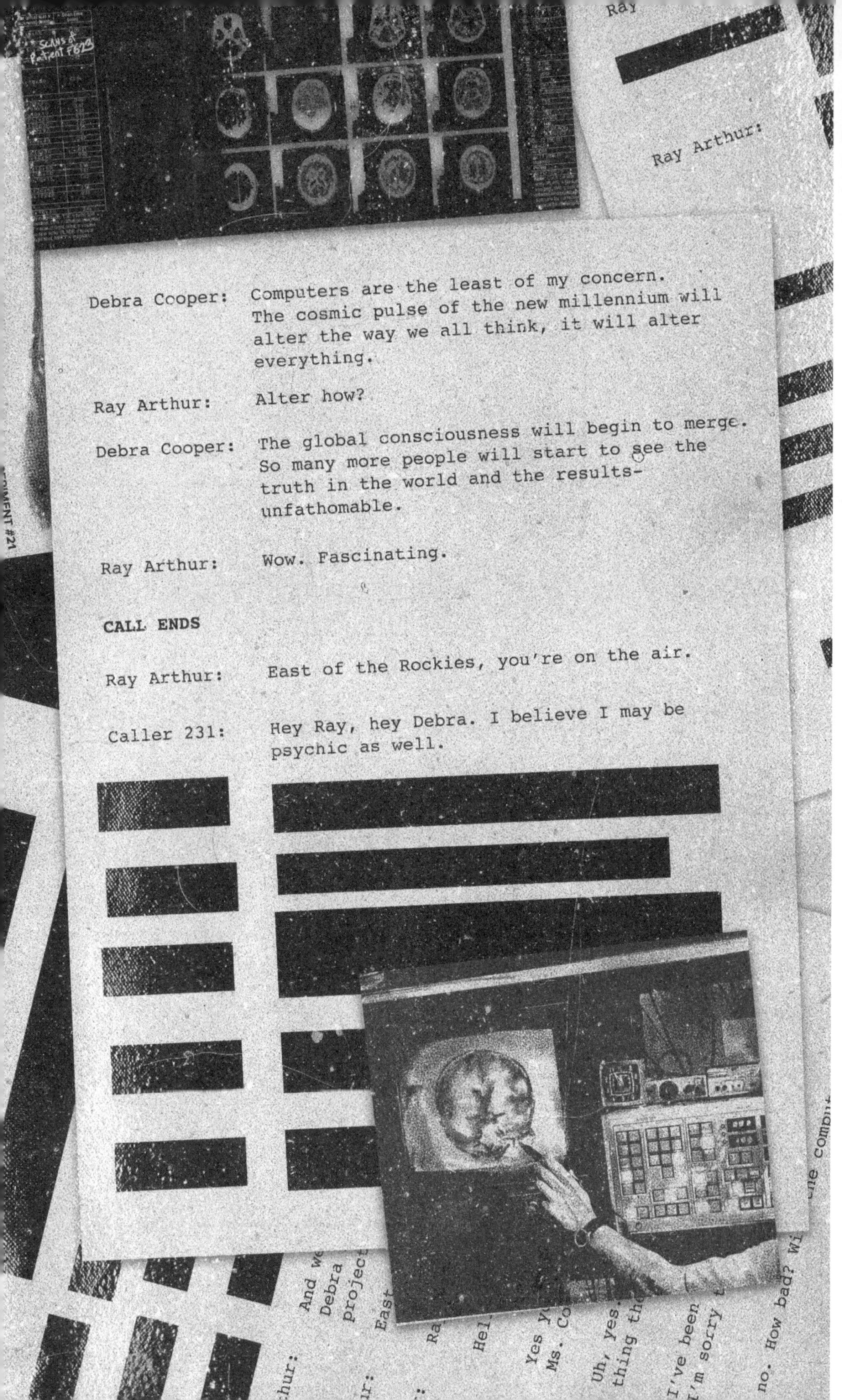

Debra Cooper:	Computers are the least of my concern. The cosmic pulse of the new millennium will alter the way we all think, it will alter everything.
Ray Arthur:	Alter how?
Debra Cooper:	The global consciousness will begin to merge. So many more people will start to see the truth in the world and the results- unfathomable.
Ray Arthur:	Wow. Fascinating.

CALL ENDS

Ray Arthur:	East of the Rockies, you're on the air.
Caller 231:	Hey Ray, hey Debra. I believe I may be psychic as well.

GOOD MORNING RAY.
HOSPITAL

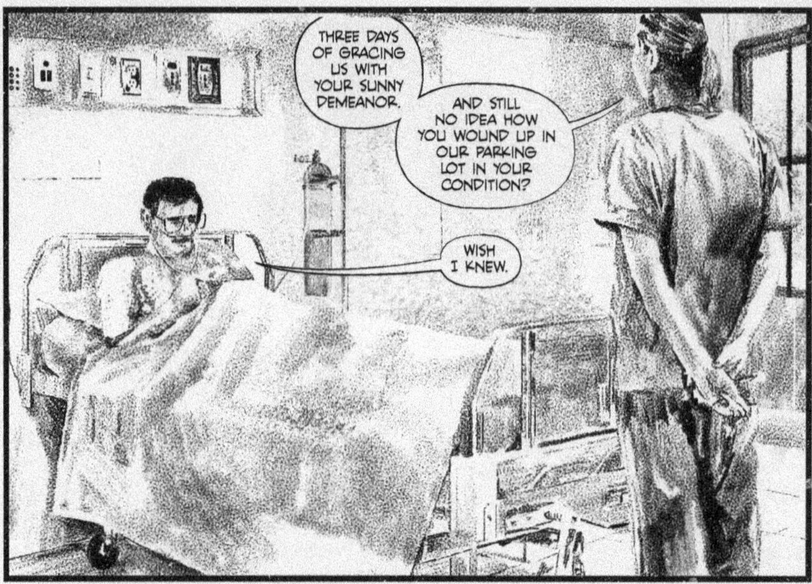

THREE DAYS OF GRACING US WITH YOUR SUNNY DEMEANOR.
AND STILL NO IDEA HOW YOU WOUND UP IN OUR PARKING LOT IN YOUR CONDITION?
WISH I KNEW.

How do you move on from that?

Do you run to the newspapers, screaming about aliens?

Do you put on a sandwich board and harass people on the street?

HOW DO YOU FEEL TODAY?
FINE.
I NEED TO CHECK MYSELF OUT.
Do you call into my show?

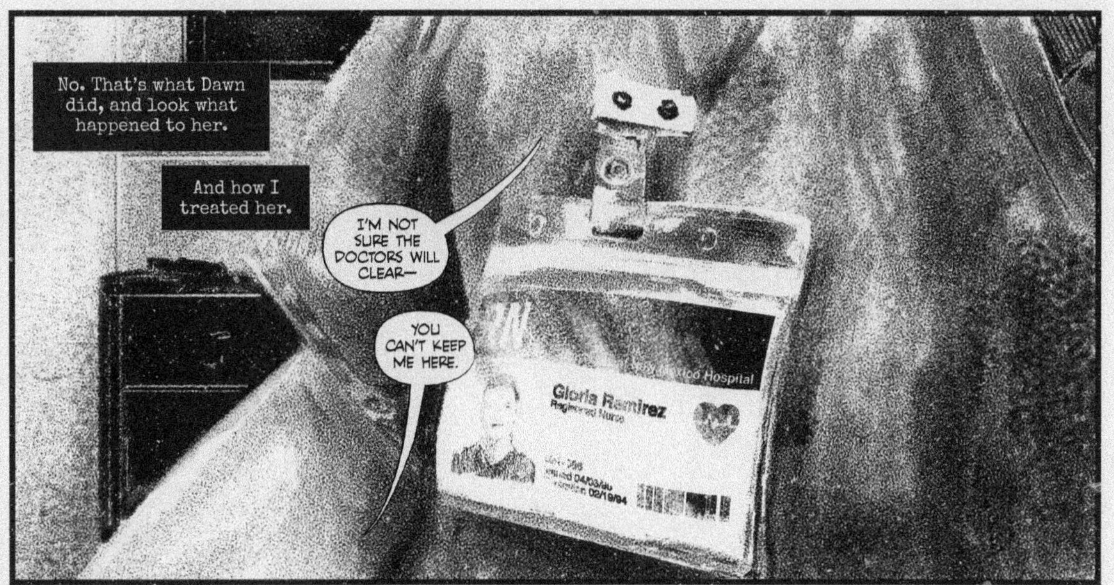

No. That's what Dawn did, and look what happened to her.
And how I treated her.
I'M NOT SURE THE DOCTORS WILL CLEAR—
YOU CAN'T KEEP ME HERE.
Gloria Ramirez
Registered Nurse
Hospital

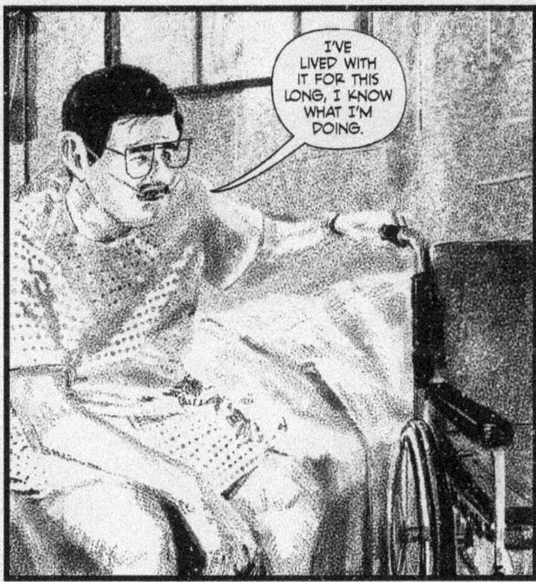

I'VE LIVED WITH IT FOR THIS LONG, I KNOW WHAT I'M DOING.

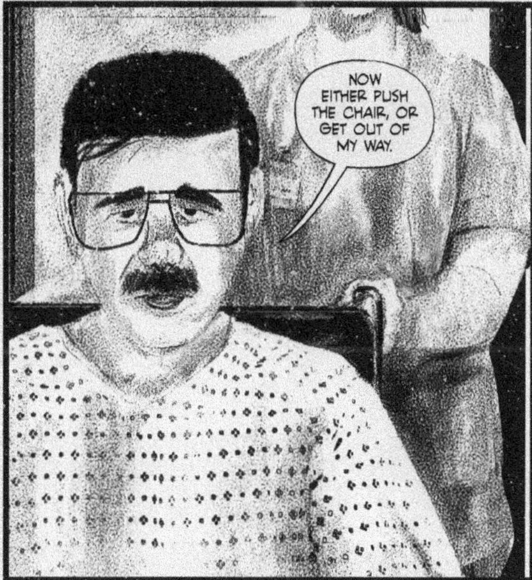

NOW EITHER PUSH THE CHAIR, OR GET OUT OF MY WAY.

WHERE CAN I GET A CIGARETTE?

FROM THE HIGH DESERT AND THE GREAT AMERICAN DESERT IN THE SOUTHWEST, I BID YOU ALL GOOD MORNING OR GOOD AFTERNOON, HOWEVER IT MAY BE.

I'D LIKE TO WELCOME BACK OUR GUEST. HE'S GOING BY "OLIVER" FOR HIS AND OUR PROTECTION. OLIVER, CAN YOU TELL US WHY YOU'RE HERE?
THANKS RAY, IF YOU REMEMBER MY LAST CALL, I HAD FOUND A HOLE ON MY PROPERTY. ROUGHLY 50 FEET AROUND AND DEEPER THAN I CAN SEE.

My first episode of Lights in the Sky made me have a panic attack.
OF COURSE.
SOME OF YOUR CALLERS RECOMMENDED I DROP A CAMERA ON A ROPE IN, AND I DID.

I've never told anyone that.
OH?
IT WAS JUST BLACKNESS ALL THE WAY DOWN, I EVEN REPEATED THE EXPERIMENT WITH A FLASHLIGHT ATTACHED BUT ꝋHEHꝋ I DROPPED THE ROPE.

The only thing that could calm my nerves was smoking.
YOU ARE KIDDING.
I WISH! AND THAT 200 YARDS OF ROPE JUST FLEW TO THE BOTTOM WITH IT.

As soon as I put one down, I lit the next.
DIDN'T EVEN MAKE A THUD!

But now? They feel like nothing.
I JUST WANT TO FIGURE OUT WHAT THIS THING IS! IS IT A PORTAL TO HELL? A BLACK HOLE? I NEED SOME ANSWERS, RAY!

I might as well be smoking licorice.
HOW ABOUT WE SEE IF SOME CALLERS CAN ANSWER THOSE QUESTIONS?
ABSOLUTELY.

This is a whole new level of panic.
EAST OF THE ROCKIES, YOU'RE ON THE AIR.
HELLO, AM I ON THE AIR?

PLEASE TURN OFF YOUR RADIO.
SORRY ABOUT THAT. SO THIS HOLE, HAVE YOU CONSIDERED RENTING A CRANE?

The unknown is still unknown.
I'D PREFER TO KEEP THE PAPER TRAIL TO A MINIMUM ON THIS. I DON'T WANT ANY BLACK SUITS SHOWING UP.

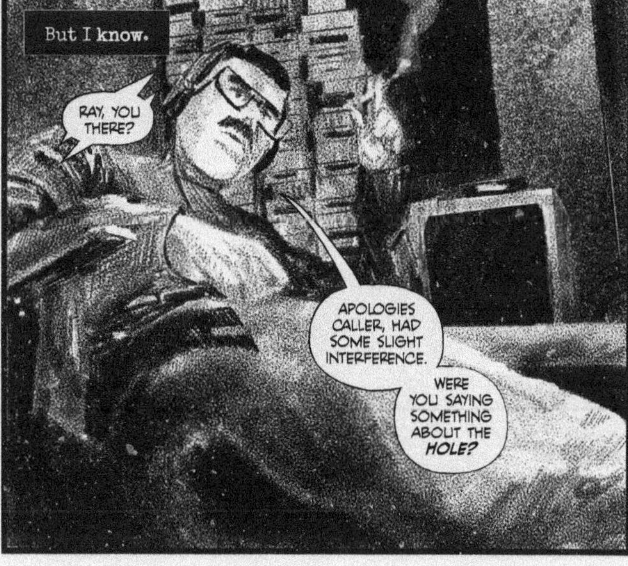
But I know.
RAY, YOU THERE?
APOLOGIES CALLER, HAD SOME SLIGHT INTERFERENCE.
WERE YOU SAYING SOMETHING ABOUT THE HOLE?

IT APPEARS SHE'S DISCONNECTED. MOVING ON...

CALLER, YOU'RE ON THE AIR.

SORRY, NO FAXES ON THE CALL-IN LINE.
WEST OF THE ROCKIES, YOU'RE ON THE AIR.

I KNOW I'VE HEARD THAT SONG BEFORE.
HELLO, WEST OF THE ROCKIES, YOU'RE ON THE AIR.

WHAT IS THIS? AM I BEING PRANKED?

DAWN?

CAN YOU HEAR ME
YES! YES, WHERE ARE YOU!?

WITH CIVAL I'M SCARED TO
H-HOW ARE YOU TALKING TO US RIGHT NOW? DAWN, CAN WE HELP YOU GET HOME?

THEY NEED ME
WHY!? WHY DO THEY NEED YOU?

AS A GUIDE
A GUIDE? BUT YOU'RE JUST A KID, A-
THE COMET IS LEAVING

I HAVE TO GO NOW
DAWN, NO STAY ON THE LINE!
DAWN!

DAWN!

≈COUGH≈
DAWN!
≈HACK≈
≈COUGH≈

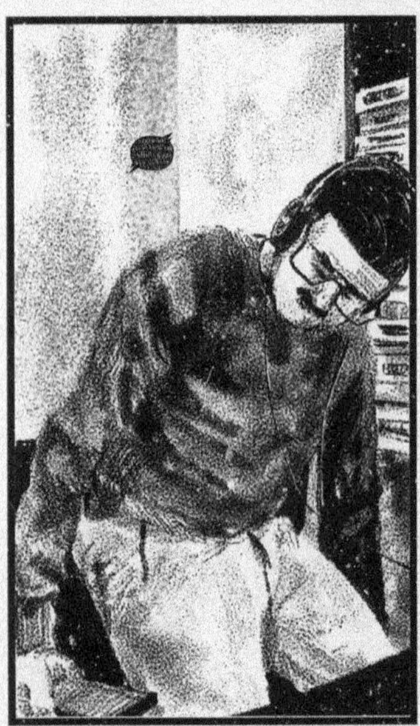

LISTENERS, I APOLOGIZE--
≈COUGH≈
THAT WAS... PERSONAL.
THE SHOW WILL BE WRAPPING UP A BIT EARLY TONIGHT, I APOLOGIZE FOR THE ABRUPTNESS.
≈COUGH≈
≈COUGH≈

WHEREVER YOU ARE, I HOPE YOU HAVE A GOOD NIGHT AND...

...STAY SAFE.
≶COUGH≶
≶COUGH≶

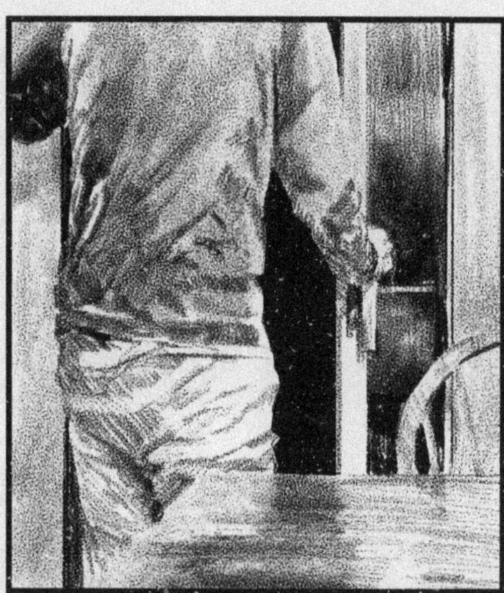

WHY HER!?

YOU WANT A GUIDE?
THEN YOU NEED-

Oh.

I know what
I have to do.
My whole life, my gut has guided me.
Joining the military, traveling the world, launching my show.
I know what I have to do.

But I've felt aimless for the past...

...decades.

But not anymore.

It was all leading to this.

It feels like a
lifetime since
I've been here.
I'm sorry,
Dawn.

I'm sorry for
what you've gone
through.

I'm sorry for how
I treated you.

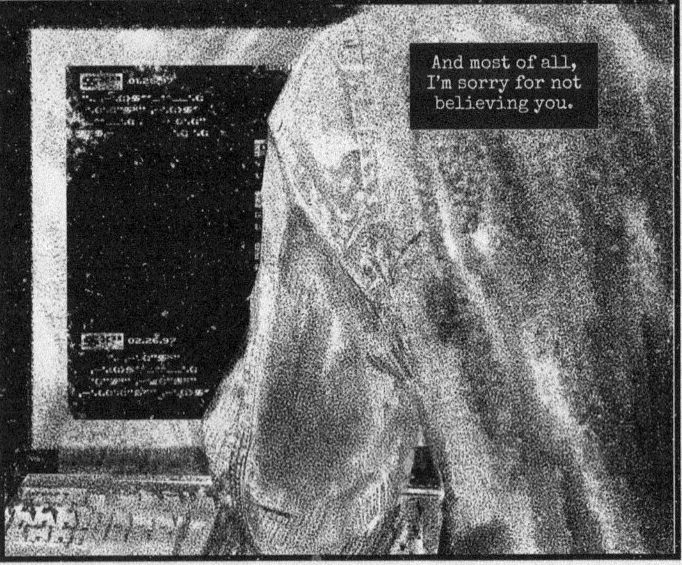

And most of all,
I'm sorry for not
believing you.

BACK
SPACE
I hope this makes
things right.
ENTER
7

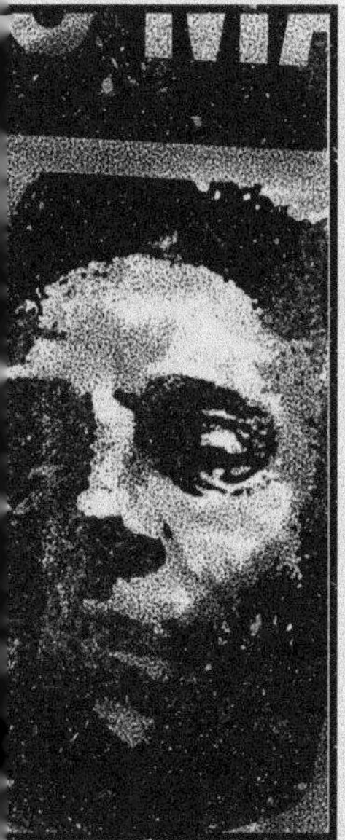

DO YOU KNOW THIS MAN?
INFORMATION
910-232-18

DAWN!

DAWN, ARE YOU HERE?
MR. ARTHUR?

MR. ARTHUR? IT'S REALLY YOU?

VAL SAID YOU CONTACTED US—
HIM AND— AND THEY DON'T NEED ME.

WHAT'S GOING ON?
THAT'S SOMETHING I'M GOING TO FIND OUT.

I OFFERED VAL AND HIS PEOPLE A TRADE.
THEY'RE LOOKING FOR A GUIDE TO EARTH.
THERE'S NO BETTER GUIDE THAN ME, I KNOW EVERY WEIRD NOOK AND CRANNY OF THIS BLUE MARBLE.

MR. ARTHUR, YOU CAN'T—
I NEED TO.

I'M TIRED OF LIVING MY LIFE WITH QUESTIONS. IT'S TIME I GET SOME ANSWERS.
KEEP LUCY SAFE.

GOODBYE, DAWN.

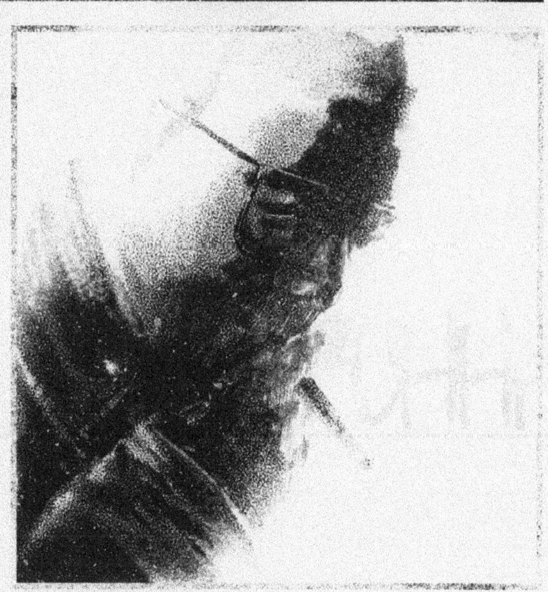

Years ago, I was struggling to come up with a name for the show.

But I remember being in a plane, back from— well it doesn't matter.

I was staring out the window and gazing into the night sky, as my eyes trailed down.

YOU KNOW THI

RMATION
32-16

I realized I couldn't tell where the stars ended and the city lights began.

It just made me think.

What if someone up there is looking for us?

What if they just see stars...

...all they see are
lights in the sky.

Lights in the Sky and Ray Arthur are satire of **Coast to Coast AM** and **Art Bell**, respectively. It's a radio talk show most known for not screening calls, and because of that, turning into an open season for fans of high-strangeness and the paranormal. What started as a political show, soon turned into interviews with psychics, alien experts, and bigfoot hunters.

The **abduction of Betty and Barney Hill** is often credited with popularizing the alien abduction phenomenon. Both of the Hills didn't remember the specifics of the event, but under hypnosis, recalled meeting aliens, getting experimented on, and being shown a star map of the alien's home planet. Betty did some speaking engagements about her encounter in her later years.

Cattle mutilation is the odd phenomenon of finding various animals (not just cattle) maimed, but often with body parts removed and bloodless excisions. In many cases, the injuries are nearly surgical. Explanations range from humans and animals to aliens and the chupacabra.

Crop circles were seemingly disproven in 1991 when two hoaxers stepped forward and took credit for the elaborate patterns. However, many aren't convinced and believe - though they may created some of the UK circles - the phenomenon is something more. Possible something non-human.

The **Planet X** (or Nibiru) conspiracy theory claims that there's a secret planet in our solar system on a collision course with Earth. The government hides it, so the general public doesn't panic at our imminent doom. Like most things of this nature, the deadline for the collision keeps getting pushed back. Beginning in 1995, tying into the Mayan 2012 conspiracies, and finally ending on "TBD".

These were both actual calls I've heard on *Coast to Coast*. How time travel wouldn't work because the Earth wouldn't travel with you, and that JFK getting assassinated was revenge from Marilyn Monroe (who apparently survived an assassination attempt).

One of the few "fun" mysteries found in this comic, **Geedis** is a cartoon character from a pin and sticker sheet labeled "The Land of Ta" featuring various fantasy heroes. The mystery stems from the fact that internet sleuths quickly realized Geedis and friends did not appear in any other media or merchandise. After years of research, the artist of the original sticker set was identified as Sam Petrucci, known for original box art on *G.I. Joe*. However, the creator of the pin remains unknown, as of this writing.

Jack Parsons was a rocket engineer, and Thelemite occultist. That opening should tell you I can't summarize his life in this short section and still do him justice. He was a strong believer in "magick" and using it to control the world around him (often under the guidance of his mentor Aleister Crowley) as well as being one of the most important people in the history of the U.S. space program. The podcast, *Last Podcast on the Left*, did a great series on him, while suggesting his magic may have allowed aliens to visit Earth.

In 1959, nine experienced hikers died mysteriously in what came to be known as the *Dyatlov Pass Incident*. In the dead of night, something caused the hikers to cut their way out of the tent, remove their clothes and run into the darkness. They were all found dead; some missing parts of their body, some dead from physical trauma, and others from hypothermia. Explanations range drastically from an avalanche, "katabatic winds", or even military involvement.

One of the most famous cryptids, **Mothman** was first seen in Point Pleasant, West Virginia in 1966. Described as a giant flying man with glowing red eyes, the monster was seen by dozens of people in the town. A month after the first sighting, a nearby bridge collapsed, killing 46, this led to the belief that Mothman was somehow responsible or possibly a harbinger of doom. In more recent times, a Mothman has been sighted in Chicago, Illinois. It is currently unknown if it's the same creature from 1966.

Sighted in 1977, the **Dover Demon** is a large-headed creature with "tendril-like fingers" and glowing eyes. It was seen twice in one night in the town of Dover, Massachusetts. The first witness claims, "I, Bill Bartlett, swear on a stack of Bibles that I saw this creature." Skeptics believe he may have seen an owl (which are commonly mistaken for aliens, if you read enough of these stories).

The Fresno Nightcrawlers are bizarre cryptids caught on camera in 2010. They seem to merely be a pair of pants walking on their own, which is actually a lot creepier than it sounds. Explanations range from children playing with their pants pulled to their shoulders, a hoax, or some sort of bird walking like a crane (no, I don't understand that explanation either).

The Hayes gas station is named after **Derek Hayes**, host of the *Monsters Among Us Podcast*. A modern day successor to *Coast to Coast*, it features call-ins about aliens, ghosts, bigfoot, and all things strange. Notably, it seems to have uncovered the "mirrored men" phenomenon. Meaning men in matching outfits and synchronized movement (much scarier than it sounds, I understand my description sounds like backup dancers).

Polybius is an urban legend of an arcade game that would somehow cause the player to become addicted to the gameplay and play to the point of insomnia and hallucinations. The story continues that "men in black" would periodically take data from the game to analyze the effects. However, there is no proof an arcade cabinet with this name ever existed.

The Impending is inspired by Art Bell's book **The Quickening.** In the book, Bell "predicts how human relations, business, technology, health, international tensions, and religion will be different in the millennium, and describes how society can prepare for the future". In my quest to read Art's autobiography as research for this comic, I was instead sent *The Quickening* FOUR TIMES. I still own two of them, and they're both signed by Bell himself.

Val is named after **Valiant Thor**, an alleged alien visitor to Earth in the 1950s. Valiant Thor came with a message of peace, and even spoke to multiple figures in the U.S. government. Photos of him are available, and he looks remarkably like a blond caucasian man for a Venusian.

The man depicted in this billboard is better known as the **Somerton Man,** an unidentified individual whose dead body was found on an Australian beach in 1948. Interest grew in the case as more bizarre elements of the case came forward, including a unique code, a scrap of poem found in his pocket, and an unknown cause of death. During my time writing this comic, it looks like the case may have been solved, and has a very anticlimactic ending (I'll leave it for you to discover it).

Only seen once in 1973, one of the most unique cryptids, **the Sandown Clown** could best be described as a combination of a clown, a robot, and an alien. Speaking through some sort of microphone system, "Sam" (as it called itself) spoke to two children that discovered it and discussed drinking from a nearby stream and eating berries. When asked what it was, Sam confusingly replied it was "all colors", it avoided most questions with an ominous "you know". The children (and sole witnesses) still claim this encounter to be true.

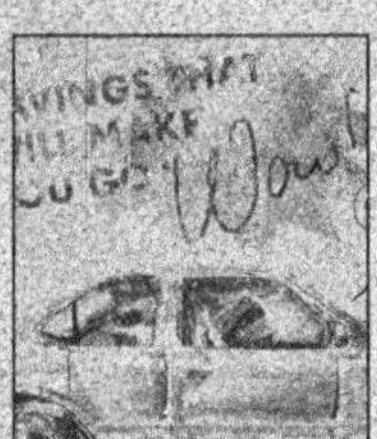

This truck's logo is a reference to **the Wow! Signal,** a radio signal from space that might be the best argument for intelligent life in the cosmos. I'm not smart enough to understand it, but it involves the scientist writing "Wow!" on the sheet and circling some numbers. Big if true.

Dawn's books are all famous books within the world of high strangeness. **Communion** is based upon the writer's personal encounters with aliens. **Mothman Prophecies** is a first-hand report about the Point Pleasant cryptid and the odd events surrounding it. The **Sirius Mystery** and **Chariots of the Gods** are both well known for pushing the "ancient aliens" theory of our history being sculpted by extraterrestrials.

The Denver Airport has a shocking amount of conspiracy theories attached to it. Best case scenario, it has terrible decorating (there are actual gargoyles over the luggage claim) and worst case, it's a homebase for the lizard people. From a realistic standpoint, it may be a bunker for government officials in case of disaster.

The story Ray mentions in this panel, is (allegedly) true! In 1896, it was reported that two men were in some sort of aircraft and struggling to keep it aloft through pedaling. A witness heard one of them yell "avoid the steeple!"

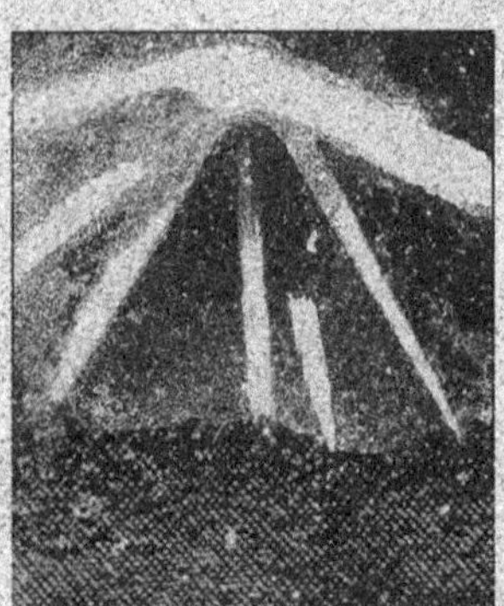

The Battle of Los Angeles was an alien sighting over the city, it scared the military so much, they fired into the sky. However, it's more likely just an anxious United States at the peak of WWII shooting at clouds. There's a very alarming photo often attached to the story, however this was touched up by the papers at the time to look more intimidating than it actually is.

12-15 blueish-green 'goblin-like' creatures reportedly harassed a family in their Kentucky home in 1995. They were shot at, but all bullets seemed to ricochet off them. These creatures came to be named the **Hopkinsville Goblins**. Skeptics believe that these "goblins" were nothing more than horned owls and claimed the witnesses had been heavily drinking.

These books all reference different media that inspired my love of high strangeness and mysteries, as well as other famous books from the world of the weird.

The Files of Why is based on **The Why Files**, a terrific YouTube series by AJ Gentile, an incredibly well-produced and entertaining show about the mysteries surrounding us.

The Malacetic Atlas is a fictional book from the podcast **Tanis**, by Terry Miles. Miles has the amazing ability to mix in unconnected mysteries to one solid narrative, all in one beautiful ambiance.

Intruders: The Incredible Visitations at Copley Woods is a famous book about one woman's encounters with aliens.

One of the best-known abduction stories, **The Walton Experience** details one logger's disappearance at the hands of a UFO as his coworkers watched. It was turned into a movie called *Fire in the Sky*.

Unexplained is based on the podcast of the same name by Richard Maclean Smith. Smith is a master of sculpting real-life mysteries into relatable and haunting narratives.

The writer of the fictional book Encounters is Marcus Park, a host and head-researcher of the previously mentioned, **Last Podcast on the Left**. They do incredible deep dives into all things macabre while keeping you laughing.

Tales from the Vortex is a shout-out to Walt Flanagan, the host of the comedy podcast **Tell 'em Steve-Dave!**. Flanagan has a passion for the supernatural and famously had a "vortex-specialist" on the show as a recurring guest.

Lore is based on the podcast of the same name by host Aaron Mahnke, Mahnke has become a podcast juggernaut thanks to his ability to dredge up forgotten stories and little-known mysteries.

Batboy Lives! Is a real book on my shelf, a collection of **Weekly World News** articles, a fake comedic periodical you used to be able to find at grocery stores.

The nurse is named after **Gloria Ramirez**. In 1994, Ramirez was being treated for late-stage cervical cancer when members of the medical staff began passing out after interacting with her. For years, It was unknown what caused the staff to lose consciousness, but is now believed that Ramirez self-treated herself with dimethyl sulfoxide, and through a series of complicated chemical reactions, she accidentally exposed the staff to dimethyl sulfate - a poisonous agent.

In Art Bell's auto-biography, he spends an unusual amount of pages describing what women he's attracted to and his ideal woman being **Shannon Doherty**. He liked her so much he kept a photo of her on his desk while he worked.

One of the most famous calls to *Coast to Coast* was regarding an endless hole on a man's property that would come to be known as **Mel's Hole**. Mel Waters, the owner of the hole, appeared on the show on three separate occasions to talk about the mysterious pit on his property, as well as the government's interest in it. Unfortunately, there seems to be no evidence of an endless hole of Mel Waters ever existing.

Several other mystery references were left out of this section due to size constraints. Find them all and let me know if you solve them!

Winston Gambro

Date of Birth:	████████
Citizenship:	████████
Height	████████
Weight:	████████
Hair Color:	████████
Eye Color:	████████
Current Residence:	████████

Winston Gambro is a Chicago based comic creator and designer currently working for Oni Press.

He's created the cyberpunk-mystery *Overflow*, the all-ages action comic *Rex Radley: Boy Adventurer*, the horror-romance, *Haunted House: A Love Story*, and has written the comedy-mystery *Gumshoe City*.

He currently lives with his cat, **Hazel**.